MURDER BY MASSAGE

STUART R. WEST

ISBN 978-1-63789-617-4
Gordian Knot is an imprint of Crossroad Press Publishing

For information address Crossroad Press at 141 Brayden Dr., Hertford, NC 27944
www.crossroadpress.com

Cover art and design by David Dodd

First Crossroad Press Edition - 2023

Dedication

I know I'm beginning to sound like a broken record (anyone remember records?), but this book is dedicated to my two loves, Cydney and Sarah, who constantly encourage and surprise.

And special thanks to Heather Brainerd, the excellent author with an eagle eye.

Chapter One

"Mommy, you said this was gonna be a steak-out!" Justin squirmed in his seat, a case of "Restless Kid Syndrome" peering out the back window. "But I don't see any grills. Or steaks or hot dogs!"

"Oh my God! You're so dumb, Justin!" His older sister Nikki rolled her eyes, a performance worthy of a teenager rather than her seven years status. Zora knew her troubles with *that* one were only beginning.

"Hush, Nikki! Don't be mean to your brother!" Zora adjusted the lens on her camera, zooming in on Room #112's door. The Dew Drop Inn was hardly the best motel in town, let alone a place she wanted to have her entourage of children hanging around. Even cockroaches would be afraid to enter the dank rooms and they can survive a nuclear blast. But her husband Phillip wasn't holding up his end when he agreed to watch the kids several days a week. She envisioned a throw-down later that evening, one where noses—Phillip's—would be bloodied if necessary.

"But, Mommy, I'm bored! Bored, bored, *bored*! I'm so bored I—"

"Enough, Justin! Mommy's working! Don't make me come back there!"

"But you promised we were going to a steak-out! I'm hungry!"

Zora tossed a box of emergency rations—sugar-packed cereal—to the back seat. Probably not the best idea. All she needed was for her little beloved monsters to get amped up on sugar. But desperate times call for desperate measures. "Knock yourselves out, kids. I mean…really, if you want to knock yourselves out, have at it."

Justin shredded the box, digging for sweet treasures. Between mouthfuls, he mumbled, "You said it was a steak-out."

"Different kinda stake-out, honey. Now, quiet…let Mommy work."

"Yeah, Justin…don't be an idiot all your life," said Nikki. "Mom's staking out a criminal. It's what she does. Gawd!"

"Is it a bank robber, Mommy?"

"No, not a bank robber."

"Did he kill someone?"

"No." *God, grant me strength. Strength to murder Phillip when I get home.*

"Is he a tellerist?"

Nikki belted out a shriek. "Sooo stupid! It's 'terrorist'!"

"I'm gonna terrorize you kids if you don't hush!"

"Mommy, Samantha just spit up!"

Oh, for God's sake. "Terrific. Nikki, clean her up."

"But, Mommm—"

"Just do it!"

"Gawd! I'd rather be back in school!"

"How's military school sound?" That always shut them up, a good and healthy fear of the American military system.

She couldn't blame the kids, not really. Phillip? Him she could blame.

They'd been parked in the lot for forty-five minutes, the weather sweltering outside. Zora'd watched her target enter the motel room, but nothing else had happened. Not quite the glamorous occupation she'd imagined when she'd hung out her private investigator plaque. Especially with the kids in tow. At least her newborn, Theresa, was blissfully asleep. Wouldn't be for long, though. Death, taxes and Theresa's unfailing hunger: three unstoppable forces.

A junker of a Celica pulled up in front of Room #112. A very familiar looking Celica. The engine kept kicking after the ignition was turned off, matching Zora's accelerated heart-rate.

No, no, no! Are you kidding me?

The driver left the car, strutting toward the door. A strut she knew only too well, putting the cocky into swagger. Her buffoon of a stripper brother, Zach.

"Crap!"

"Mommy, the swear jar!"

Rather than argue with her kids how "crap" hardly constituted a full-on curse, she tossed a quarter in the back seat. Bigger fish to fry and such.

Zach. Of course. Of all the sleazy ports to dock in, it really shouldn't have come as a surprise he'd wash up on shore here. His non-stop libido acted as a trouble magnet, driving him toward the worst scenarios possible. And now here the idiot was, setting himself up to be implicated in an adultery case. For a brief moment, Zora considered shuttling the evidence, not taking the photo. Leaving Zach out of the mess.

The hell with it.

Her brother always decided which slutty bed to ruffle, so he could lie in it.

Click, click…

Zach rapped on the door, dug his hands into his jeans pockets. Looked around, smiling for God's sake, the whole world his audience. He knocked again. Then he opened the door, poked his head in. And vanished inside.

"Was that Uncle Zach, Mommy?"

"'Fraid so, Justin."

"Is he here for a steak?"

"Sort of."

Seconds later, the door flew open. Zach staggered out, hand over his mouth. He pitched forward, vomiting by the door.

"Ewwww! I don't want steak anymore!"

"Quiet, Justin!"

Something was wrong. Detective's intuition. Or just the fact Zora'd seen her brother respond this way before. Usually when something bad had happened. As it always seemed to do when he showed up.

"Nikki, watch the kids! Lock the doors!"

Before her daughter could answer, Zora zipped out of the car, the camera bouncing on a strap around her neck. Zach had dropped to his knees, hands on the sidewalk. Still spewing. He might've had abs of steel, but a candy-assed stomach.

"Zach?"

He looked up, eyes glassy, complexion lighter than his usual store-bought tan. "Zor? What're you doing here?"

"Probably bailing your butt out of trouble again. The hell's going on?" Although Zora already knew.

Zach hitched a thumb behind him toward Room #112.

Zora withdrew her gun from her jacket pocket. Carefully, she tapped open the door with her toe. "Hello? Miss Meadows?" She jumped in, swinging her gun in a wide arc. The room was empty.

Except for Mrs. Meadows's corpse lying on the bed. Fully dressed and in peaceful repose. Her hands were folded over her chest as if a mortician had given her an early-bird discount. If it weren't for her whiter-than-bone color, she could've been napping. Zora double-checked, found no pulse.

"I've got a gun! And I'd kinda like to use it!" Zora edged toward the bathroom, although she expected to find it empty. Better safe than dead, though. She kicked in the closed door. Yanked back the shower curtain. The bathroom window stood open, a moth-chewed curtain flapping in front of it. She stuck her head out the window, looking into an empty back alley. Perfect for the killer on the run.

Nothing else in the room looked disturbed, no signs of a struggle.

Outside, Zach was still hacking like a cat with a hairball, now suffering the inevitable throes of dry heaves.

Zora stood over him, arms akimbo. Ready to kick ass. "Zach?"

"Yeah?" He looked up, framed a feeble smile.

"Why in the *hell* do you keep *killing* people?" She felt like adding a kick to his behind. But there's no sense in kicking a dog when it's down.

"What? Wait...you don't *really* think—"

"No, I don't think you killed her. But this is the *second* dead body you've found in a year! Do you have any *idea* how that's gonna look to the cops? So why are you even *here* in the first place? To get your rocks off and—"

"Zora, no! It's not like that! Misty was...my massage therapist!"

"Wait...she was a masseuse?"

"No. A massage therapist. Highly skilled in the art of—"

"Uh-huh. Just like you're not a stripper."

He sighed, already over his trauma. Nothing fazed him more than defending his sleazy occupation. "I'm a male entertainment dancer! I've told you, like, a million times!"

"Yeah, yeah, yeah. And I'm a fairy tale princess just living the dream. Where'd I park my unicorn? Tell me what happened. Don't leave anything out. And get up already."

Zora shielded her eyes against the sunlight, and glanced at the car. Three of her kids were plastered to the windows like attentive dogs. Probably getting pretty hot in there.

Zach clawed his way up using room #112's window sill. "I had an appointment with Misty. For my monthly massage and—"

"Were you sleeping with her?"

"What? No! It wasn't like that! You know dancing can be hard and stressful! I know I make it look easy, but—"

"You mean sleazy."

He ignored her. "Really, dancing takes its toll on my body temple." He splayed hands over his body, gave a little flex. "To keep in such perfect shape, Misty's talents helped to loosen me up. Work the kinks out."

"You've got more than a few kinks to work out. What time was your appointment?"

"One o'clock."

Zora checked her watch. "It's 1:15 now. Anyone else know about your...appointment?"

Zach squinted, trying to dust off his rarely used grey matter. "No. No, I don't think so."

"Okay. So you showed up here and..."

"Well...she didn't answer so I went inside. I saw her on the bed, thought she was asleep. So I—"

"Crap. Tell me you didn't touch her."

A corner of his mouth hitched up, his disarming grin. Zora wasn't buying it, locked and loaded with dwindling patience. "Yeah...I shook her. Thought she'd fallen asleep. Like I said. Duh."

Her hand flew up and hit the back of his head.

Swak!

"Ow, dammit! Why'd you *do* that? I've been through a terrible experience! I—"

"Didn't you learn anything from last time? Anytime you find a dead body—like that should happen to anyone, even once—you don't touch it! *Duh!* You may as well go in there and roll around next to her now that your DNA is all over—"

"I really don't wanna do that, Zora."

She counted to ten, expelled a heavy sigh. Not for the first time she wondered if one of them might have been adopted.

Zach plucked out his phone, looked at the time. "Hey, I really gotta get goin', Zor. I got a gig tonight."

"*What?* You've *gotta* be kidding me! You're not going anywhere!"

"But…I'm headlining tonight."

"You can strip any time, Zach! You're not gonna run like you did last time! This time we're doing things by the book!"

"What if they arrest me? You've gotta help me! I'm too pretty to go to prison!"

"Yeah, 'pretty' something. If you want my help, we're going through the proper channels." Before he could whine anymore, Zora dialed 911. She turned her back on his protests, hurriedly giving the details. "They'll be here in a bit. So…if this was a straight-up 'massage,'" she hooked finger quotes, "why were you meeting in a sleazy motel?"

Zach scratched his head, flipped a lock of hair behind his ear. "Well, you know, Misty…um, it was her idea. She didn't want her husband to know she was a massage therapist."

"Why? If she was on the level?"

"Beats me…I think…maybe she was kinda afraid of him. Or something."

Huh. Hardly the impression Zora had of Martin Meadows…

Two days ago, a light rap as weightless and inconsequential as the man behind the hand sounded at Zora's office door.

"Come in!" Quickly, Zora swept her legs off her desk, spread papers out and buried her face in them. Best to look busy.

"Um…hi…" With a comb-over as wispy as webs, and glasses like magnifiers, Zora immediately pegged him as an accountant. Sure, she was stereotyping but some stereotypes are labeled for a reason. "Is this…ah…the LeFevre Detective Agency?" He looked around at the nearly barren office, then stared up at the ceiling as if expecting a Divine answer.

"That's what it says on the door."

"You're…you're a…woman."

"*What?* When did that happen?" Zora stood, visually explored her body.

"Um…"

Zora nearly laughed, probably not a great idea. Clients were pretty sparse. "Come in, have a seat. I'm Zora LeFevre, private detective. Is my being female going to be a problem?"

"Oh, no. No, no, no, not at all. I just…"

"I know, right? Were expecting a man? Believe me, I've got credentials. Surely you researched me."

"Well, no…I saw you were offering a Groupon."

He may as well've slapped her in the face. It pained her to resort to such shameless marketing ploys, but it had drawn in a few clients. Cheapskates, but clients nonetheless. "Fine. And you are…?"

"Oh, my. Where are my manners?" He sat, fidgety and scratchy as a tweaker. "I'm Martin Meadows." He blinked, blinked again, a nervous Morse Code. Waiting as if his name should mean something.

Clearly she'd have to take the lead. "And what is it I can help you with, Mr. Meadows?"

Grumble, brumble, rumble….smack, cackety-cack!

The small lamp on Zora's desk wobbled, the pull-chain clanking against the body.

"What in the *world* is that, Ms. LeFevre?"

Zora shrugged. "They're bowling below us. You get used to it after a while." Again, Zora wondered who thought it was a good idea to lease office space above a bowling alley. Hardly instilled confidence in clients. Still, even Sam Spade started in run-down offices.

"I...see. Anyway...it's my wife. Ah..." He adjusted his glasses. Took them off, wiped them with his tie. Zora sincerely hoped he wouldn't cry. Her job description didn't extend to "mothering" overwrought men. She had enough of that at home with her husband.

"Go on, Mr. Meadows."

"Here..." He snapped open his briefcase. Slipped a photo across Zora's desk. Practically a glamour shot, a woman with platinum-blonde hair straight out of a film noir from the '40s. And way out of Martin Meadows's league. He either had a tiger in his tank or a whale of a bank account. "This is my beloved. Misty Meadows."

Zora fought the urge to roll her eyes. "Mr. Meadows...is that her *true* name? I mean...no offense, but it sounds like a...stage name." Actually, a porn name, but clearly tact was needed here. Mr. Meadows appeared so frail, he might blow away if Zora sneezed.

"Yes, I can assure you it's her real name. You see, Misty had...ah, different kind of parents."

"Ah, yeah, that's something I can identify with, believe me."

With seriously pursed lips, he studied her as if waiting for enlightenment. "Be that as it may...I believe..."

Time to kick-start her client. Sometimes they just needed someone to say it for them. "You believe she may be cheating on you?"

He dropped his head, ashamed that his poor, fragile male ego had taken a beating. "Yes," he peeped.

"I understand, Mr. Meadows. This is a tough time for you." He nodded, his practically non-existent chin melting into his neck. "But I have to ask some questions. What makes you think your wife is being unfaithful?"

"Well...several times I've called her from work. From the accounting firm." *Aha! Score one for stereotyping!* "And she doesn't answer the land-line. Other times...when I contact her via her cell phone, it sounds like she's out."

"And where does she say she is?"

"Shopping. Always, always shopping."

"Some women shop, Mr. Meadows. Wish I had time to do it more often."

"Wahhhh, wah, wahhhh!"

Meadows jumped at the sudden sound. "What in Heaven's name?"

Crap. Theresa, the queen of terrible timing, had arisen. Zora swooped her baby up from the portable carrier at her feet, stood, and swayed back and forth. "Shhh. It's all right, Theresa. Go back to sleep." Like preaching to an atheist when her youngest was hungry.

Meadows ran a finger around his tight collar, gulped. "Um…if this is a bad time for you, Ms. LeFevre, I can come back."

"No, no, no. Sorry. I feed her full, it'll knock her right back to slumber land."

"Oh. Oh, my!" He held a hand over his eyes, looked as if he might faint.

"Ah, Mr. Meadows? Don't worry, I'm not breast-feeding."

"Yes…well, then…" His cheeks burned red as a fire engine. Briefly, Zora wondered what kind of sex life the Meadowses had. Then quickly erased the scarring imagery from her mind's chalkboard.

Zora kicked the mini-frig open, grabbed a bottle. "Here you go, Theresa. Eat like the wind."

Swoop, shp, slurrr…

"Sorry for the interruption, Mr. Meadows. As I was saying, shopping's hardly an indictment of adultery." She rocked her baby back and forth, while impossibly reaching for a professionally serious demeanor.

"I understand that. But…there've been other clues. Lately, she's not been putting as much effort into dinner. As if it's a last minute, microwave decision."

Talk like that made Zora want to kick him to the curb. She'd heard the same ridiculous accusations hurled at her by Phillip. Just because it's a man's world didn't mean she didn't want to burn it down. But she held her tongue. "Does she work?"

"No. There's no need for her to do so. I make a fine living." For the first time, he smiled, proud of his accounting hoo-hah.

"Any children?"

"No, I'm afraid not. Nature has deemed that impossible for us, sad to say." And his conquering-hero persona vanished. He ducked back into cleaning his glasses.

"Have you considered she might be bored? I'm not trying to sound callous or uncaring...but if there aren't children and she has no job...what *does* she do with her time?"

Zora put the bottle down, grabbed a burp pad, and lifted Theresa to her shoulder. "That's what I'd like you to find out for me, Ms. LeFevre. I believe...she's lying to me. Perhaps...having an affair. I've even noticed...several motel bills on the credit card."

"You ask her about those?"

Brrrrrp!

"Oh, crap...sorry." Zora glanced at the white glob Theresa spat up on her shoulder, trying to ignore it. "Did you ask your wife about the motel room charges?"

"No, I didn't."

Theresa conked out. Zora dropped her into the carrier and resumed her seat, considering the best way to handle the wallflower in her office. "Look, Mr. Meadows, are you sure you want to find out the truth? I ask this of all my clients. Some of them change their mind, preferring to go on living their lives."

Meadows leaned forward, his eyes narrowing. "Oh, no. I wouldn't be here if I didn't want to find out the truth." For a moment, she glimpsed something else in his eyes, something cold. Typical cuckolded husband behavior? Or something darker? Then he slipped back into mild-mannered accounting mode. "You see, I love her so very much."

"I know you do, Mr. Meadows."

Grumble, brumble, timble....snakt, ka-chak, spak!

Zach stood outside the motel room as the two uniformed cops kept glaring at him, experts with the evil eye. Too bad the way they wore their uniforms was pathetic. A disgrace, really. Their clothing draped loosely, not a muscle in sight. Zach sometimes thought he'd make a great cop should he ever hang up his banana hammock. He'd look damn fine in the outfit, saving damsels in distress and reaping the rewards. Probably needed to quit stumbling across dead bodies, though, before he took the oath of lawfulness.

"Zora, how much longer we gotta hang out here? My gig's in—"

"You know what, Zach?"

"What?"

"Shut up, that's what. In case you hadn't realized it, you're a person of interest."

Person of interest? Usually, Zach would take pride in such a title. After all, he was the most interesting person he knew. But the way his uptight sister said it? This kinda interest he wasn't so much interested in.

"But I didn't do anything! I just—"

"Zach, I know 'shut up' is like a foreign language to you. But do try and brush up on it."

"Right."

His nephew and nieces had joined the waiting party, more bored than he was.

Nikki had her phone out, ready to go viral on the crime scene. A girl after his own heart. As they say in show business, any publicity is good publicity.

"So…there's a dead person in the room, Uncle Zach?" Nikki asked.

"Yep. Deader than disco."

"I don't even know what that is. But I wanna see the dead body!"

"Me, too," said Justin.

Zora tossed an arm around the two, corralling them closer to her. "Um, yeah, not gonna happen. What happens at the Dew Drop Inn, stays at the Dew Drop Inn."

"Sorry, kids." Zach tossed his hands out along with a smile. "You really don't wanna see her. Kinda messy."

"Whoa! I really wanna see now," said Nikki.

Zora shot Zach her killer look, one he always seemed to be on the receiving end of. "Hey, just tryin' to help."

"Help like yours I can do without." Zora squinted, staring at a Cadillac pulling into the lot. "Oh, crap…"

"What, sis?"

"It's Soundtrack Saul."

"Soundtrack...what, who is he? A talent agent or something?" Zach brightened. Maybe the day wouldn't be a complete wash after all.

"No, he's not an agent! Gah! Now be quiet. Let me do the talking. We're gonna be here a while. And whatever you do...don't say *anything* about his behavior."

"His behavior? What? Is he gonna waterboard me or something?"

The Caddy tilted down as a large man stepped out. His donut of hair supplied the icing on his well-donut-fed belly. He hitched up his suit pants high, way too high, higher than men did in '50s movies.

Suddenly, he stopped, twirled.

"Ba-boom, gadda boom!" He halted, took a quick step back. *"Ka-cha!"* Then repeated his self-supplied chorus along with three mincing steps forward, one awkward hop back.

"Ba-dang, buh-boom!" In a squat, his hands crossed and splayed like a blackjack dealer. He bounced up, gaily strolling. Terrible dance moves.

"Who's the cop who pulls out the stops? Saul! Who's the cop who solves every crime? Saul!" His singing voice was nearly as bad as his dance steps. *Almost. "Don't do the crime if you don't want the time! Ka-chow! 'Cause Saullllllll! Ol' Saul's on the case!"* For his big finish, he lifted a foot, twisted, landing in a "he's safe" umpire position. *"Look out!"*

Clearly here was a man who could benefit from Zach's expertise. "Um, hey there. You know you could really use some dance lessons. Just so happens I'm a famous, expert male dance entertainer and *oooffff*!"

Zora's elbow dug deep. But her menacing glare stabbed worse. Zach mouthed *"What?"*

The big man strolled up, pulling at his trousers which had ridden low. Not once did he take his gaze off Zach. Zach's testicles retracted a bit.

"Hey there, Saul," said Zora.

"Zora. Long time." He still only had eyes for Zach, practically ignoring his sister. "What's the story?"

"Um, yeah. Dead one inside. Masseuse by the name of—"

"A massage therapist," interjected Zach.

Saul's eyes narrowed. Somewhere Zach thought he heard a spaghetti western theme twanging away, foreshadowing an impending showdown.

"Uh-huh. And who's this?" Saul jerked his chin toward Zach.

"Saul, meet Zach. Zach, meet Detective Saul Jenkins."

Zach extended his hand. The detective left him hanging. Instead, he wrangled his trousers up again. Tough crowd.

"Um, nice to meet you, Detective Jenkins. I was—"

"Why's he here, Zora?"

"He discovered the body. He had a 1:00 massage appointment scheduled. Walked into the room and found her."

"Oh?" Twin, white clouds of eyebrows floated up on Saul's forehead. "I…see."

Zach thought he wasn't really seeing, not one bit. "Um, yeah, I walked in and there she was. Dead. I thought she was asleep so I shook her and—"

"Uh-huh. Before you killed her?"

"Wait…no! Course I didn't kill—"

"Uncle Zach! You killed a lady?" cried Justin.

"Quiet, Justin! Zach didn't kill anyone. Look, Saul, I know it looks bad. But I can prove Zach didn't do it."

"Uh-huh. And how can you prove that, Zora? Seems to me like you're a little biased in this case."

"I took a photo of him entering the room." She lifted the camera from her chest. "It's time-coded. Once you find out the time of death, he'll be exonerated."

"Sounds…kinda iffy."

Crunch, runch, cranch…

Gravel crunched beneath the detective's feet as he invaded Zach's personal space, way too up close and uncomfy. He huffed, a two pack-a-day wheeze whistling from his nose. A strong scent of jalapeno and onion made Zach nearly gag. "What was it you said about my dance steps?"

Got him. Now just to reel him in.

"Well, not that your moves were awful or anything…" Saul took an even closer step, their noses practically touching. "…um, no, I can see some real talent there. Somewhere. You just need refinement. Was that a moonwalk you were going for?"

"Something wrong with my moonwalk?"

"No, no, no! Not at all! I just—"

"Hey, Saul," said Zora, "how 'bout you take a look at the crime scene? Maybe you can—"

"What's wrong with my moonwalk?"

"Hey, I thought it was a great moonwalk! It's just...well, maybe you've heard of me, the Banana Hammock Bandit? I'm a famous male entertainment—"

"A stripper." Saul worked his lips, spat a wad of chewing tobacco to the pavement.

"Um, no, actually I'm a male entertainment dancer. I just thought, you know, I might—"

"Oh, for God's sake, Zach, shut up already! Saul, I'm sure you can see something inside that I couldn't and—"

Saul ignored her, Zach the only one in his world now. "You actually think you can teach me a thing or two." He chortled.

"Well, yeah. I've got the moves of an angel. Fast, smooth and—"

"A murder suspect." Quicker than a man of his size belied, he whipped out cuffs and spun Zach around.

"Hey! Hey, what the hell're you—"

"Shut up, stripper-boy. I'm taking you in for questioning."

"Saul, you're making a mistake," said Zora. "He didn't do it! You can't just arrest him based on—"

Saul shrugged. "Not arresting him. Just taking him for holding."

"Uncle Zach's goin' to prison, Uncle Zach's goin' to prison, Uncle—"

"Quiet, Justin! Saul, just let me show you the photo I took and—"

"We'll sort it out down at the station, Zora. But right now? Pretty boy's being held." He turned Zach around to face him. "Show you to comment on my moonwalk," he grumbled.

Saul stormed toward the motel room, stopped. He bent his knees, started shuffling gravel back in a pathetic moonwalk.

"Tump…timp… Oooooooh!" The high pitched squeal hurt Zach's ears more than the tight cuffs. *"The stripper is not my frienddd! Ooooh! I'll see justice done in the enddd! Hooooo!"*

Out of breath, he stopped in front of Zach. "Talk about my moonwalk now, why don't ya?"

"Um…it was fantastic, sir! Best moonwalk I've ever seen! I couldn't have done better, not in a million…no, a trillion years! It was—"

"Yeah. 'S'what I thought." He gave a knowing nod and a smile.

"Okay, Saul, you've proven you're the best dancer in the Dew Drop Inn parking lot. Now how about letting Zach go?"

"Sorry, Zora. Ol' Saul has to see justice done."

It'd all happened so fast. Zach couldn't believe it. He was going down for a crime he didn't commit. "Zora!" he screamed. "You've got to help me! I'm too pretty to go to the Big House!"

"Oh, for God's sake."

Not exactly the response he'd been looking for from his sister.

Chapter Two

"Sing another song, Saul!" Justin shook Saul's arm, rattling him like a maraca.

Good. If her kids were annoying enough, perhaps Saul'd give up in exasperation and release Zach. For once, their brattiness might prove to be a benefit. If only she could cage the tiger when not needed.

"Zora, you sure that's everything?"

"Come on, Saul! Sing more Michael Jackson! Just one more song. Please? Pleassseeeee?"

"For God's sake, Zora!" Saul shook Justin off like an annoying gnat, not far from the truth. "Can't you keep a lid on your..." He stuttered, waved a hand throughout the station, at a temporary loss for words. *"...kids?"*

Nikki had embarked upon an exploratory mission, touching everything she could break and asking endless questions. Like a miniature shadow, Samantha toddled along behind her. Mercifully, her angel, Theresa, chose to sleep through the hour-and-a-half ordeal.

"It's out of my hands, Saul." Zora couldn't help but smile. "As soon as you release Zach, I'll get them outta your hair."

As if seeing if his hair was still (partially) there, Saul ran a hand around his rim, leaving it poofed out at the sides of his skull. He sighed. Still not ready to throw in his "big stick. So...what's your take on Martin Meadows?"

"Just one more song? Puh-leasseeeeee!"

"Indoor voice, Justin. Meadows is hardly the murderous type. Sort of a wallflower. A little strange, really."

"Strange?"

"Not strange in a sudden psychopath rage kinda strange, but…sort of a relic. I mean, he got really embarrassed when he thought I was gonna breast-feed."

Saul shook his head, his eyes springing wide. "Um…you're not gonna—"

"Gah! What is it with you men? We've got a dead body on your hands and everyone's freaking out I'm gonna flop out my boob or something!"

"Mommy, you said boob!"

Zora fished into her purse, pulled out a dollar bill. "Here, put that in the swear jar. There's gonna be more coming. Or go get a soda or something." Get 'em even more sugared up. That'll show the cops to mess with a mother of four.

Justin zipped off, blindly bouncing into a woman cop. "Nikki, Nikki, I'm getting a soda! You don't get one!"

By the water-cooler, Nikki called out, "Not fair. Mommmmmm!"

Saul glared at the speeding torpedo. His walrus mustache fluffed up when he snorted. "So, you don't like Martin Meadows?"

"Didn't say that. Of course you should talk to him. But he just didn't strike me as the killing type."

"Not even a crime of passion?"

"Saul, the guy had the passion of a celibate monk. But, again, it's the meek ones you have to watch out for. Now…quid pro quo…what can you give me?"

Saul grinned, a knowing, cocky grin Zora associated with the men's club in blue she used to deal with. "You're not privy to that info, Zora. You know that."

"My case. Martin Meadows brought me into it. Furthermore, you've made me a huge part of it by locking up my brother. Who, again by the way, didn't friggin' do it! You know that, I know that. Let him go."

"Still got questions for him."

A time-killing tactic, nothing more. "That's a load of crap, Saul. Here…" Zora flicked through her camera's photos until she came across Zach entering the motel. "Look…1:06. Misty Meadows was dead long before that."

"Time of death hasn't been established yet."

"Fine." She thumbed through the camera's screen again. "Here's when Misty entered the room. 12:30. Trust me, no one else entered the room. Someone else was already in there, waiting for her. And, clearly, they escaped out the bathroom window."

Saul leaned back in his chair, the springs creaking like a frog. Twisting his mustache, thinking.

Gotcha. Even Saul couldn't be foolish enough to ignore hard evidence.

"We both know electronic surveillance can be rigged with false results."

"Uh-huh, right. And when would I have had time to do that? Between discovering a dead body, watching over four little monsters and my goofy stripper brother? Come on, Saul!"

"Zora, you and I've crossed paths a couple times in the past when you worked security for Denham and True. I know your reputation. I don't know your…stripper brother's."

"Then do it as a favor to me. Release him. I'll stake my rep on his innocence."

"He had motive, opportunity—"

"What motive? Because he wanted a damn massage?"

"I'm considering it."

"Consider it a little faster. Unless you want my miniature terrorist squad to destroy your precinct. Now…I can help. And since my brother's involved now, if you think I'm gonna back down, you don't remember me. What can you tell me?"

Saul moved his fingers across his keyboard. As he rocked back and forth in his seat, he started singing. *Of course.*

"Ol' Saul knows where to look. Ka-chow! Can read a crook just like a book. Ba-Bam!" Suddenly he stopped. Unusual. "Hmmm…"

"'Hmmm,' what, Saul?"

"Nothing…just interesting. That's all I can say." Truly enjoying the moment, he challenged her with a grin.

"Spill, Saul. Remember…I can help. You'll get all the credit, of course."

He sat back, hands enfolded over his belly. "Sorry. You know the rules, Zora. What can you tell me about Misty Meadows?"

Okay. He knows something about Misty that I don't. "Not much, really. Trophy wife, I'm thinking. Didn't work. They couldn't have kids."

"Oh? His fault or hers?"

"I dunno. God's, whatever. Anyway…that's about it. Except, of course, I found out she's been working as a secret masseuse."

"Secret? Why secret? Hooking on the side?"

"Not from what Zach tells me."

"Back to him again. How do we know he's not lying? To protect himself?"

"Oh, for… Do you really think he's smart enough to lie convincingly?"

"Suppose not. So…no 'happy endings'?"

Zora grimaced. "No. No happy—"

"Mommy, Mommy, who's getting a happy ending?" Justin bounded up, now wearing half of his grape soda. "Is Uncle Zach getting a happy ending?"

"Ah… We hope so? But let's not talk any more about happy endings. Let's just drop it and call it pretty."

Saul's phone rang. "Hang on a minute. Homicide… Uh-huh…"

Zora drew Justin in close. Time to play sneaky. "Justin, you remember what Mommy taught you?"

He thought for a minute. Licked his lips, took a swig of soda. Sugar his petrol, his eyes lit up. "Shock and awe?"

"Yep, honey, shock and awe. Go practice on Detective Saul."

Absolutely shameless, she knew. But she'd learned how to harness her weapons of mass destruction to her advantage.

Excited, Justin set the soda can on the edge of Saul's desk. Warily, Saul eyeballed it, scrunching up a bit in his chair to see if any had spilled. Justin ran behind him, merrily swinging his hands.

"Saul, Saul, Saul! Look at me! I'm an airplane bomber. *Nrrrrrrrrrr….atta, atta, atta….Boom!* Look at me, Saul! *Rrrrrrrrrrr…*" With his arms stuck out, he strafed Saul, dodging in and out and letting his vocal bombs fly close to the detective's ear. Saul swatted the air, trying to attend to his call. "I'm a airplane with bombs! *Rrrrrrrrr.....boom, ka-boom!"*

Zora caught Justin's eye, nodded. Covert for "time to land."

With a smile, Justin stuck a well-trained foot beside Saul's chair's back wheel and fell on his hands. Perfect landing. At the top of his lungs, he screamed. Brought on the crocodile tears. Zora couldn't have been prouder.

"Saul tripped meeeeeeee!" Justin shot the stymied detective a horrified look before racing off through the station.

"I've gotta call you back." Saul fumbled the phone, hung up. Glared at Zora as he took off in hot pursuit of Justin. "Jesus Christ, Zora!"

As soon as Justin led the pursuing detective far away, Zora shook Saul's mouse, reawakening his computer screen.

A mug shot of a much younger, very different looking version of Misty Meadows, under the name of Melissa Saunders. Brunette and pissed at the world, a hard life lived. Arrested as a teenager. In the '80's, she took part in a radical anti-nuke protest. The group she was affiliated with, Benito's Bandits, brought bats, chains, other non-ballistic weapons to a rally with the express intention of causing property damage. Didn't really matter that it was a business office building. Zora supposed they were excited about small-scale damage, just couldn't stomach the bigger stuff like nukes.

As Saul had said, this *was* interesting.

Crap, crap, crap…

Big trouble. Zach looked around at his fellow holding cell inmates, a scary looking bunch. Some guy in the corner kept laughing to himself, an inside joke Zach wanted to stay far outside of. A couple of brutes with beards hanging down to their elbows watched him, daggers in their eyes. But Zach'd been around, a worldly guy. He'd seen prison movies.

The way to remain safe? And not made into a love slave? Especially for a pretty guy such as himself? Gain their respect. *Bingo!* He had something to offer them, something they'd kill for. On second thought, that was a poor choice of words. But best to be proactive.

He took a deep breath. Clapped his hands. "Guys! Guys, if I could have your attention please!"

Bird's Nest Beard turned, fists coiled, ready to spring.

Tear Drop Tattoo said, "Why you pressin' us, amigo?"

"Hey, no pressing here, fellas! I'm just gonna let you in on a little secret."

"Yeah," said Beard part #2, "you gotta escape plan?"

The men roared. But in moments, Zach knew, they'd be roaring along with him, not at him.

"No. Something much better. How would you guys like to know the secret to picking up women?"

"What're you? Some kinda self-help guru?" asked Top-Knot. He nudged his partner-in-crime, Pockmarks. Batman's villains had nothing on these guys.

"Better than that, my friends. I…" He waited, building suspense. What show business is all about. "…am a male entertainment dancer!" Zach stuck out a well-muscled arm, twisted, ending with one ankle across another.

"What? You mean a stripper?" Some of the men laughed, but Zach could see he had the attention and respect of others. Just not his usual type of audience.

"Well, no…a male entertainment dancer."

"Like…ballet or some pussy crap like that?"

"Not exactly…I…" The hell with it. He hated referring to himself as a "stripper." So crass and below his artistic prowess. But when in Rome… "Okay, sure, I'm a stripper."

"You gay?"

"What? Course I'm not! Otherwise how could I teach you to impress women? Duh."

"I dunno…sounds kinda'…artsy fartsy," said Bird Nest.

"Thank you! It is an art form. Really!" A few men groaned, showing a lack of appreciation for culture. He needed to show, not tell. Fast. Before things turned ugly. "Okay, let's start with my power song, my jam!" The record spun in his head. The beat developed. He bounced on the balls of his feet, winding his arms back, pumping them forward and clapping to the beat. "Come on! Join me, guys!"

Clap…clap…clap…

Nothing. He needed to make them feel the song, live the energy. "Ladies and gent….um…gentlemen and gentlemen! Please welcome…the Banana Hammock Bandit!"

Instead of the wild applause he usually earned, some guy in the back asked, "Like the puppet guy on the McDonald's commercials?"

"No…that's, um, a different guy." *Get to it already, Zach! You're losing them! Bad showmanship, bad!* "One, two, three!" *Clap, clap, clap… "Come on, feel the noiseeee! Girls, rock your boys! We'll get wild, wild, wildddddd…"* The Beard Brothers started bobbing their heads. A calculated move on Zach's part, he knew they'd be part of the Quiet Riot posse. *"…wild, wild, willllllld!"*

Zach tore off his T-shirt. Spun like a dervish. The shirt whipped over his head, a cotton lasso. He tossed it to the chortling old man in the corner. "Santa Claus! *Catch!*" Santa caught it, sniffed it. *Ewww.*

"Come on, guys! You know the song! Now *feel* it!" Zach moved, liquid lightning. He turned around, his back to his fellow cons. On retrospect, it might've been a bad career move. Exposing his goods to lustful minds. But too late, the zone had taken him. He leaned forward, extending his legs out. Farther, farther… Slapped his butt, began his club-shaking tremors. He felt his butt muscles trembling, strong as an earthquake. He bent down, looked between his legs.

Hard to tell when the men appeared upside-down, but more seemed to be bouncing their heads in a laid-back manner. Some started swaying, singing along. *Success!* The hardest show he'd ever played. But audience involvement is everything.

"*Come* on, guys! You want the ladies?"

"Yeah!" Bird Nest pumped a hand. When in prison, always sidle up to the biggest guy.

"You guys wanna get some *somethin'-somethin'*?"

"Hellz *yeah*!"

"Then show me what you got!" Zach straightened, started prancing around the cell, weaving in and out between his fellow suffering inmates. "Second verse! You guys know it! *So you think I got an evil minddddd! I tell you honey I don't know why! I don't know whyyyyy!*"

"*Why, why, whyyyy!*" The Beard brahs supplied a shockingly angelic chorus. Bird Nest swayed his hips, pumped his arms in a frightening, violent manner.

"That's it, Bird Nest!" Zach hopped over to the T-shirt-sniffing Santa in the corner. "You! Santa Claus! Use what God's given you!" When Zach slapped Santa's bulging belly, the sound thunked like a ripe watermelon. "Move it! Round and round! Just cause you're round, doesn't mean there's not a lady out there somewhere for you!"

Santa continued laughing at his private joke, drool running down his beard. But he took Zach's advice, twisting at the hip and rolling his hands over his impressive stomach.

"That's it! You!" Zach pointed at Tear Drop. "I know you've got some impressive moves in you. Show us what you've got!"

Tear Drop didn't disappoint. While not Zach's style, he started free-styling, pulling some damned impressive and quick moves. Before long, he was on the cement, break-dancing. No one likes a show-off. "Okay, that's enough from you, Tear Drop. Get up and give the other fellas a chance."

Zach raced up to the thin, twitchy guy in the corner. He dropped to his knees, sliding toward Twitchy, arms out and offering the secret to success. "*So you think my singing's out of time! It makes me money! I don't know why! I don't know*....um..." Twitchy beamed off into another world, scratching and staring at the wall. Not the best of students. "Okay, moving on!"

Half of the men were on their feet, dancing. A rag-tag chorus line, but frankly close to a miracle. "Yeah, boys! Keep it up! *So, come on feel the noise! Girls, rock your boysss! We'll get wild, wild, wilddd! We'll get wild, wild, wilddd!*"

Zach surveyed the group, proud of his work. Time for the big finish. "Alright fellas..." The thundering drumbeat lowered in Zach's zone, hushed and dramatic and ready for him to divulge the eighth wonder of the world. "...what I'm about to show you is my specialty. It's what made me the man I am today! No one else at the Bone-In Beef

Club has mastered this stroke. And this will seal the deal on any future dates! You guys ready?"

A few grunts, the men too involved in their own private dances.

"I said, are you guys *readyyyyy*?"

"Yeah!"

"That's more like it! Alright, everybody follow my lead." Again, he turned his back to them, this time fully confident they'd leave his assets untouched. He curled his fists. The shakes started in his lower leg muscles, worked up to his calves, then his rear. Shaking like the guy in the corner. "This is the build-up! The big build-up! Pretend your body's a stick of dynamite!"

"Right on!" Apparently, some guy *really* liked dynamite.

"Your fuse has been lit—by your special lady-friend..." Maybe not so politically correct. "...or, um, guy friend...now what're you gonna do with it?"

"Blow shit up!"

"Well...no...we're gonna build and build and build...you guys feel it?"

"Hell *yeah*!"

Zach's whole body shook, energy barely contained and straining at the edges of his body temple. The zone owned him. "Get ready for it guys! I said get *ready*!"

"We're *ready*!"

"Here it comes! Do what I do! Exactly how I do it!" He pushed his hips back. Brought his hands up to his chest. Shoved his waist forward with all his might. *"Boom! Sonic pelvic thrust!"*

Zach felt his energy blast off, the next best thing to sex. Around him, the men must've felt it, too. Laughter, loud singing, a series of vocal explosions.

Like a ringleader, Zach proudly paraded around the room, high-stepping, directing his acolytes in a rousing final chorus. Over and over again.

"Come on feel the noise! Girls, rock your boysssss! We'll get wild, wild, wildddd! We'll get wild, wild—"

"What in the holy *hell's* going on in *here?* It's like some kinda damn girl scout talent show of somethin'!" The guard stood before the door, key in the lock, jaw unhinged. No doubt blown away by Zach's talents.

But it was enough to douse the men's lively routine. Some groused back to their corners. Only Santa kept up the singing and clapping. Between his guffaws, naturally.

The guard shook his head. "Swear to God, I gotta get a better job. Let's go, Caulfield. You're outta here."

As much as he craved it, Zach didn't wait around for his due appreciation. Freedom tasted better. "Sorry, boys, gotta run." He snatched his shirt back from Santa. "Keep up the good work, Santa. Beards! Work with it. With lots of practice, some day you'll hit it big."

"Hey! Can I try out at the Bone-In Beef Club?" asked Tear Drop, the show-off.

Zach waited until he was on the other side of the closed gate to answer. "Sorry, Tear Drop, some guys just don't have what it takes."

When he turned back around, he nearly ran his sister over. And the spectacularly untalented Soundtrack Saul.

Zora sighed, shook her head, said, "You done playin' with your new little friends yet, Zach?"

Voices rose in the front lobby of the police station. Dreaded and all-too-familiar voices. Hand on hip, Zora turned to her brother. "Zach! Tell me you didn't call them!"

"Hey, I know my rights, sis. One phone call. And I was kinda scared so—"

"So you called our parents, for God's sake? Our hippy, '60s-stuck, police-hating parents? Hellooo! Not a good move! Why didn't you just order a pizza or something?"

Zach looked aghast at the idea. "Zor, my body's a temple! I'm not gonna defile it with artificial—"

"I'm gonna turn marauding colonialist on your temple! Gah! Now I've got another fire to put out."

They pushed through the door, Saul bringing up the rear. At the front desk, Zora's father, Kelp, sporting a T-shirt emblazoned with *Down With the Fascists!* was ranting and raving, waving his arms about like a man on fire. Torn between fear and embarrassment, the desk sergeant shot Saul a pleading *save me* look. Sunshine, not nearly as bright as her namesake at the moment, stood behind her husband, wringing her hands.

"What *now*, Zora?" asked Saul.

"Nothing. I'll take care of it." Zora walked toward her parents with open hands, cautiously taming a hostage situation. "Mom, Dad, settle down."

"This is an outrage, I tell you!" Undeterred and apparently not noticing Zach, Kelp continued. "Down with the pigs! The fascists can't keep my boy in jail for—"

"Dad!"

"...long! He's an artiste! An artiste, you hear me! He's a sensitive soul who'd never hurt a fly! Why he—"

"Dad! Zach's out. *Helloooo!* Right here and—"

"Oh, there you are, Zora! I hope the Kansas City pigs have come to their senses! I'm a tax-paying citizen!"

Not really.

"And my boy's an important part of the cultural community! He's an integral component of the Kansas City Ballet! He's—"

"Ummm...Zora, what's he talking about?" Saul asked.

"Just go with it, Saul." Zach still hadn't told their parents about his stripping livelihood, such as it was. One of these days, Zora intended on having a lengthy chat with them if Zach didn't come forward. Perhaps it might finally tarnish his golden halo. Doubtful. But Zora kept hope alive. "Dad, Mom...everything's fine. Calm down."

"My boy!" Sunshine swept by Zora and draped her arms around her son. "How'd they treat you? Did they waterboard you?"

"No, Mom, I'm fine." Zach flashed his pearly whites. Zora doubted he'd been to the dentist since childhood and hated him for it.

"They break any kneecaps? Beat you with a phone book?"

"Um, ma'am, we haven't had phone books in the precinct for some time," said Saul.

Sunshine wheeled on Saul, finger prodding in his face. "Don't you give me none of that technology crap, boy-o! What'd you do...put all your cell phones in a pillowcase and beat my boy with them?"

"Oh, for... Ma'am, we don't torture suspects. We—"

"He's not a suspect!"

At a loss for words, Saul sought refuge the only way he knew how. He spun so fast Zora thought he might break a hip. Then he eked out a stuttering, nervous singing voice. *"To be determined, to be determined, to be determinedddd..."*

"The hell's this?" hollered Kelp.

"Dad! Quiet. *Please.* Let me handle this."

"Zora, this is what makes this country so rotten to the core! Corrupt pigs railroading innocent citizens into—"

"Zora, can you *please* take your family reunion elsewhere? Before I change my mind about your brother?" Clearly exasperated, Saul ran his hands through his little remaining hair.

"You hear that, Dad? They're gonna throw Zach back into the can unless you settle down!" Zora pointed out the door. "Go wait for us outside. *Now.*"

"But...but...this is an *outrage!*"

Good Lord. Worse than my kids. Speaking of which...where are they?

As if dialed into the psychic hotline, her kids raced out of an office door, screaming. A first. Not the screaming, that was par for the course. But they never came when she wanted them to.

"Mommy, Mommy! Officer Bieber showed us—"

"Um...it's Bleever," said a harried female cop chasing after them.

"Well, hello there," said Zach with a wink.

Zora shoved him. Absolutely shameless.

"Grandma! Grandpa!" Justin hurled himself at his grandfather's legs, finally ending his bluster.

"Hey there, little one!" He jutted a finger out toward Justin, a joke even her kids found infantile. "Pull my finger. Go on, pull it, boy!"

Saul intervened before the toxic fallout of the finger-pulling procession could be released. "Zora! Get them out of here! Now!"

"You heard the detective." Zora pleaded with Sunshine, a marginally more reasonable voice. "Mom, take Dad and the kids outside. We'll be there in a minute."

Sunshine harrumphed, tossed protective arms around Nikki and Justin. "C'mon, Grandpa. We don't wanna get any of that foul bacon smell on us anyway." On the way out the door, she turned once more and sniffed.

"Right behind ya, Sunshine." Kelp swooped up Samantha, who had been holding her arms outstretched. They'd left behind Theresa, still blissfully asleep in her carrier seat next to Saul's desk. As quiet as she was, maybe Zora needed to rig Theresa up with an alarm of some sort.

Relieved, Saul slumped back against a desk, massaging his jowls with long strokes. No wonder they were so lengthy. "Good Lord, Zora…you put up with that every day?"

She shrugged. "I'm a warrior. Sorry 'bout that, Saul. Hey, when you hear the cause of death, would you let me know? And anything else that might be important?"

Saul shook his head. "You know I can't do that, Zora. We talked about—"

"Wait. Let me go get my parents and kids again. They might—"

"No, no, no! Oh, *hell* no! Fine. I'll call you and let you know what I find out. If it's not crucial to remain under wraps in nailing the perp." Saul eyeballed Zach.

"Hey, I didn't do it already!"

"To be determined, to be determined, to be determineddddddd!"

"Thanks, Saul."

"Whatever. But stay out of this, Zora. I mean it. Leave the investigating to the professionals."

And there he did it, pulled one of Zora's triggers as surely as firing a gun. Probably not the right time to assert herself, but what the hell. Saul opened that can of worms. She intended to Tupperware it and ship it back to the dark ages. "Dammit, Saul, I *am* a professional! Fully licensed like a big girl and everything. It's my ethical duty to follow-up with my client, tell him what I know about his late wife! Don't you dare tell me how to detect! I've helped you boys out more times than—"

"Fine, geeze, okay." The twin hands of surrender flew up. *Victory.* A small one, but Zora'd take it. "Just...talk to your client. But don't do anything else. Not without talking to me first."

"Sure, Saul, whatever you say." *But, um, not.*

"And this goes without saying..." Saul stood, hitching up his slacks by the belt-loops. Ready to launch into another routine. *"Don't leave townnnn, this helluva townnnnnn!"* With a foot lifted, he spun on the other, planting himself into a wobbly stance, finger pointed toward Zach. *"If so, I'll run you downnn, take you to groundddd!"* Big finish. "Ta-chaaaa!" He snapped fingers on both hands, slapped his holstered gun.

"Um, yeah. Listen, Detective, maybe if you loosened up a bit, lost a little weight and—*Ow!* Dammit Zora, quit *hitting* me!"

"Let's go, Zach. Bye, Detective, thanks for all your help!" Zora ran her words together quickly, and made a hasty exit before Saul could toss them both in jail. At the door, she shoved Zach into it.

Whoops.

His face squished against the glass with a satisfying splat.

"*Crap!* Really, sis, you gotta quit—"

"Saving your stripper ass? Yeah, I know. Go while I grab my second most immature kid." Zora snatched up Theresa. Still mysteriously, extraordinarily asleep. On her way out the door, Zora waved at Saul while he munched down a roll of antacid tablets. "Ta-ta for now, Saul! See you soon."

As soon as Zach stepped outside, he joined his parents, a safe harbor from Hurricane Zora.

"Still can't believe this happened to my ballet star," said Sunshine. "Are you sure you're okay, Zach?"

"The very idea, treating my son like a common criminal," said Kelp.

"I'm fine. No prob. You know me, nothing can keep me down for long."

Zora joined them, glaring as usual. His sister had some mean anger management issues.

"What exactly happened, Zach?" Kelp slapped him on the back.

"Well, nothing really. I just—"

"Uncle Zach found a dead massage lady in an icky hotel," said Nikki.

"*What?* Is that true?"

"Um, not exactly, Mom. First, she was my massage therapist. You know…I need to keep limber for my ballet performances."

"Or something like that," said Zora.

"Anyway, it was my monthly massage therapy appointment. And…she was dead when I got there."

"That's terrible! You sufferin' from PTSD, son?"

"Wait…what? No, of course not! I'm careful when I have—"

"Yeah, um, let's move this along." Zora sighed.

"Hey, I'm just wantin' to make sure my boy's fine, that's all." As Kelp gave Zach a once-over, he frowned. "Um, son? Your pants are comin' undone."

Crap. Attached at the sides by Velcro, a flap of his favorite tear-away pants hung down like a dog's lolling tongue, exposing a hip bone. Quickly he reattached them. "Whoops. Sorry 'bout that. Life in the Big House, you know." He hoped to divert, disarming them with his winning smile.

"Those are some mighty interestin' britches, son. What kind are they?"

"Um…I wear them for ballet practice. You know…ergonomic yoga pants. Yeah..."

"Might have to get me a pair of those," said Kelp.

Zora rolled her eyes. "Oh, sure, everyone at the K.C. Ballet's wearing them, Dad. You should come see Zach perform one of these days."

"Like nothin' better. How 'bout it, son?"

"Well, you know about my stage fright, Dad. Sorry." He shot Zora a look. Very amused with herself.

"That's fine. One of these days, maybe."

"Maybe." Zach kicked at the pavement.

"Leave the boy alone, Kelp," said Sunshine. "You know he's sensitive. I like your britches just fine."

"Thanks, Mom."

"Mom, Dad," said Zora, "I hate doing this, but can you watch my little ones for a while? Zach and I have some work to do."

With a look of greed, maybe Big Bad Wolf hungriness, Sunshine immediately snatched baby Theresa within her arms.

"Sure, no problem, sweetie!" Kelp whipped Justin up on his shoulders. "There's a terrific veggie bar nearby."

"*Nooo!* Mom, don't make me go! *Please!*" Nikki clutched onto Zora's shirt, pulling as if in a desperate game of tug-of-war. "*Please* let me go with you to work. Please, please, *please*!"

"Quiet, Nikki. Where we have to go isn't any place for children."

"Not fair! I don't *wanna* go to a vegetarian—"

"I wanna go to a vetchta...vegta—"

"Shut up, Justin! You don't even know what a vegetarian is! Please, Mom, I'll be good!"

Sunshine chuckled. "Now, now, Nikki." She bent over, hands on knees. "They have a great asparagus smoothie. You'll love it!"

"Mom, *noooo*!"

"It'll make you good and regular, Nikki," said Kelp.

"Noooo! Mom, I'm too *young* to be regular! My friend Nita's grandma is regular! And she has to wear plastic underwear!"

Justin's eyes lit up. "I wanna wear plastic—"

"Shut up, Justin! You wanna poop yourself? Idiot!"

Justin considered. "Kinda."

"Mom, please! I'll do dishes for the rest of my life! I'll—"

"Oh, for God's sake!" Zora tossed her hands up. "Dad, can't you make an exception? Just this once? Take 'em for a milkshake or something?"

Kelp wrinkled up his face. "Now you know that goes against all my moral fiber and—"

"Dad! So, it's okay for you to pack my kids' colons full of fiber?"

"Mommm! I don't wanna explode," screamed Nikki.

"I *wanna* explode!"

"Hey guys..." Zach ran intervention, always good with the kids. Sometimes he thought he'd make a great father. "...it'll make your pee smell funny." He winked at Nikki.

"Noooo! Mom, please!"

"Zach, you're not helping!"

"I want *my* pee to smell funny!"

"Mom, just take them to Sonic," said Zora. "You and Dad don't have to get anything. Just for a little while."

Sunshine took pity on Zora. Or more than likely wanted to get out of the heat. She looked sweltering in her massive sundress. "Oh, fine, Zora. Just lookin' out for your kids' best interests. *Someone* has to."

"And what's *that* supposed to mean, Mom?"

"Never mind. Alright, kids!" Sunshine clapped her hands. "Everyone into the love van!"

"That thing's still running?" asked Zora.

Zach wondered the same thing. Painted all the colors of the rainbow, rust had overtaken his parents' "Mystery Machine," probably the only element holding it together.

Zora looked at the beaten down van, shook her head. "Be careful with my children. And…no funny business." She held pinched fingers to her lips and sucked in.

"What? Mommm! Grandma and Grandpa smoke reefer?" cried Nikki.

Kelp appeared insulted. "Of course not!" With a shrug, he added, "Not while we're driving."

"I know I'm gonna regret this," mumbled Zora. "Fine. I'll call you when we're done. Probably take a little over an hour."

"Don't worry about us, Zora. We'll have a great ol' time!" said Kelp. "Everyone in!"

Justin shot off, screeching like fireworks.

On the other hand, Nikki trudged away, dead man walking. "Thanks a lot, Mom!"

"Don't mention it, honey!"

Zora relaxed as soon as the van ambled off down the road.

"Sis, maybe you should visit a massage therapist. You know, a living one?"

"Oh, no! *You* don't get to tell me what you think I need! If you'd quit turning up dead people, we wouldn't be here in the first place!"

"Hey, that's not fair. What—"

"And *you* think it's fair I have to keep cleaning up after you? When're you gonna grow *up*, Zach?"

"Why do you always have to be so mean?"

"Mean? I'll show you mean!" *Whack!*

"Jesus! That's what I'm talkin' 'bout!"

"Mean. You don't know what mean is," Zora growled.

"Oh really? You've always been mean. Remember back in sixth grade when you teased Suzy Whittaker and pulled her pigtails and—"

"That was you, Zach!"

"Oh. Oh, yeah. Right." Zach didn't really remember it that way. But anything to calm his sister down. "Anyway…what're we doing?"

"We're gonna go see Mr. Meadows. Have a little chat."

"Oh. Oh, crap."

"Really, Zach? *Really?* That's all you've got is 'oh, crap'?"

He had no idea what she wanted him to say. But he blurted it out anyway. "Oh, shit?"

"Give me strength…"

"I just…I just don't wanna call on a grieving widower or whatever."

"Tough. Let's go. I gotta be home by six." She kicked at the sidewalk, hissed, "Shit."

"See, Zor? Therapeutic word, right?"

Chapter Three

The Meadowses lived in a neighborhood as comfortably bland as the accountant himself. With a little help from a lazy architect, the American Dream built the suburban houses, every one practically the same and knocked out like an afterthought. Nothing about Martin Meadows surprised Zora, very easy and safe to read. She wondered if that would continue to hold true.

In the driveway, Zora cut the engine. "Remember. Let me—"

"Yeah, yeah, yeah. Got it. You'll do all the talking. I remember from last time. I'm not a baby, you know."

"Really, Zach? Huh." She turned around, scanned the back of the car laden with children's toys. "Think there's a rattle in here somewhere."

"Funny, sis. Really, why don't you let me stay in the car? I—"

"Nice try. You're not getting off that easy. If I have to face this, so do you. Besides Mr. Meadows might say something that's relevant to you."

"Cool! So I'm like a detective or—"

"Not 'cool!' Just settle down, Hasselhoff, and don't open your mouth."

"Got it already. Geeze."

Truth be told, Zora hated calling on a grieving husband as well. But in her experience, it was always the place to start. Some clichés can't be escaped. She rang the doorbell.

A woman, slightly graying, answered the door. With a librarian's demeanor, she looked down her nose through glasses and clasped her hands. "Yes? How can I help you?" Her pinched lips were pulled even tighter by her bun of hair. Apparently she'd been shopping at Ye Olde Victorian's Secret. A bow-knot clasped at the top of her throat while her shoulders poofed up like miniature parachutes. For a moment, Zora thought she'd stumbled through time, faced with a gothic, scary housekeeper.

"Um, hi." Zora offered her hand. The woman dropped her icy gaze to it, nothing else. "I'm terribly sorry to call at a time like this, but I—"

"You should be."

"Excuse me?"

"Have you no shame? Calling on my brother's home while he's grieving the loss of his wife?"

"Ah…again, I'm sorry. But that's why I'm here. I'm—"

"Hey there, I'm Zach." Of course she accepted Zach's hand. Even showed an iceberg of a smile. Just the tip. "Look, I'm really sorry. But we'd like to help Mr. Meadows in his time of need. We're, ah, special investigators. And I—"

"I'm Zora LeFevre. Mr. Meadows hired me for a case."

"I *see*." Zora could practically see frigid condensation hiss from her mouth. "You're the…private investigator."

The way she dragged out her job title made Zora feel lower than a stripper. People's priorities were way wrong these days. "That's correct. And you are?"

"Not that it's any of your business, but I'm Melora Meadows. Martin's sister." Apparently the Meadows family loved alliteration. "I'm afraid I must ask you to call again at a later date. Poor Martin's just spoken with the police and I'm afraid he's not up to company right now." Quickly, she smiled at Zach and ignored Zora, the story of Zora's life when her brother was around.

"This won't take but a few minutes, Ms. Meadows. I just—"

"Miss."

"Sorry?"

"It's 'Miss Meadows.' You called me 'Ms.' I assure you I'm not a feminist, nor am I a young trollop."

Gee, who'da guessed?

"Oh, so you're on the market?" asked Zach.

Good Lord. Surely this walking Frigidaire won't fall for—

"Why, oh my Heavens no!" She tittered. *Dammit.* "I was married once. But now I'm a widow. Even though I'm still married in the eyes of the Lord I proudly reclaimed the Martin name." She patted her bun, making absolutely no difference. Even swayed a bit, cheeks burning bright.

"You look much too young to be a widow, Miss Meadows." Unabashed, Zach grinned.

"Oh my! Thank you for the kind words, young man."

Dear God, give me strength to make it through this day…

A voice called out from within the house. "It's okay, Melora. I'll talk to them." The flirt fled from Melora's face. Grimly, she swung the door open, clearly disappointed her fantasies were stillborn. "Very well. Come in then, please."

Zora took a step in and the older woman's hand stopped her. "Ah-ah. Shoes off first, please. Cleanliness is next to Godliness."

"Of course." Zora hopped on one foot, hand on the wall, slipping out of her flats. Zach gave her a puzzled look. Like it's the first thing he's taken off in front of people.

In stocking feet, Zora followed the bouncing bun of Melora's hair down the hallway. They entered a sunken living room, Martin Meadows sinking even lower into a pristinely white couch. Other than that, he didn't appear to be in mourning, his eyes clear, the skin around them his usual shade of pale.

"Good afternoon, Ms. LeFevre. If you've come to tell me of my wife's demise, the police have already spoken to me about it."

"Ah…first of all, Mr. Meadows, I'm truly sorry for your loss. I wanted to check on you, see how you're doing."

"How do you think he's doing?" spat Melora. "The poor man's been through a great deal and you're just adding to his pain." She sat next to her brother, her bony hands kneading his shoulders.

"Come now, Melora. That's no way to treat our guests. Please, Ms. LeFevre, have a seat." He gestured toward the twin seats across from the sofa.

"Thank you." Zora saddled up. When Zach sat, the Velcro detached from the side of his pants again.

Scritch.

Martin Meadows narrowed his eyes. "I'm sorry. And you are?" He blinked rapidly at Zach, waiting.

"I'm, um, special investigative—"

"This is my brother, Zach. Unfortunately, he's the one who discovered your wife." Usually Zora would've told a white lie to protect her brother. But Martin Meadows was a client, after all. And she didn't want to kick-start her new career by lying to paying customers.

"I…see." Martin swiveled his head between Zach and Zora. Ripples formed across his forehead. Zora hoped they wouldn't form into a tidal wave of anger.

"I'm not sure how much the police have told you, but things aren't quite as they appear. Your wife—"

"I'm sorry. But are those…tear-away pants your brother's wearing?" Both Martin and his sister sat up, anticipating a suspenseful plot twist or something.

"Oh, yeah, they're—"

"Sometimes in our line of work, Mr. Meadows, we're called upon to get our hands dirty. So…we dress for the occasion." So much for not lying to her clientele. Better that, though, than have the grieving husband believe his wife had been having an affair with a stripper.

"And just how is my brother's affairs such a…'dirty' occasion." Melora said "dirty" like it pained her. Zora suspected a world of Dad's asparagus smoothies might do her some good.

"Didn't mean to imply that at all. I'm sorry. Let me start over. Your wife was at the hotel for a legit reason. She—"

"'Legit,'" sniffed Melora. "Humph."

"As far as I can tell, Mr. Meadows, your wife wasn't having an affair. She was faithful to you and—"

"And living a double life. Yes, I'm now painfully aware, Ms. LeFevre. Must we rehash this again?"

"I understand. But apparently she was a legit masseuse."

Zach held up a professorial finger. "A massage therapist."

"A massage therapist. She was licensed with several clients."

"All of which she kept from me." Martin hung his head and draped folded hands between his knees.

Of course Zora thought she'd be bringing good news. Of a sort. But Martin seemed to be taking the masseuse news worse than if his wife had been unfaithful. Tough crowd, tough crowd.

"And I presume, Zach, you were one of my wife's...clients?"

"Um...kinda."

"Kinda?" asked Melora. "How can you 'kinda' be a client? Either you are or you aren't. Which is it?" She glared at Zach. If she'd entertained romantic fantasies regarding him before, they'd long been shoved away in the cobwebby attic of her libido.

"Okay, yeah, I was a client. But I gotta tell you, sir, your wife was a great massage therapist! The things she did with her hands! Fingers of steel and—"

Zora coughed loudly, overriding Zach's wildly inappropriate testament to Misty Meadows. "Excuse me."

"I truly don't believe we need to hear all of the sordid details," said Melora. "If you're here for a reason, get on with it. Otherwise I'll ask you to leave." She held out a rigid arm, straight as an ironing board, her finger pointing toward the door.

"I apologize for my brother. It won't happen again." She shot daggers Zach's way. He mouthed "what?"

"Mr. Meadows," continued Zora, "you were married to Misty for five years. Is this correct?"

"Yes."

"Might I ask where you two met?"

"Online. A Christian dating service. The Christian Cuddle Corner."

"Praise Him!" As if in ecstasy, Melora closed her eyes, raised a hand. Martin followed her lead. Silence filled the room.

The Martins stayed that way for an uncomfortably long time. Zora feared they'd fallen asleep. Finally, Zach raised his hands and yelled, "Praise Him!"

"Indeed," said Melora.

Hands dropped, eyes opened. Back to business.

"Um, yeah, praise him," said Zora. "Mr. Meadows...how much did you know about your wife prior to your marriage?"

"Honestly, this has gone about far enough," said Melora.

"It's okay, Melora." Martin tamped his hands down. "Just what Misty'd told me. She was a farm girl, brought up as a God-fearing Christian."

"Praise Him!"

Zora sighed, but played along. The only way to get information from them apparently. "Yep. Praise Him. Did you know anything else about her prior life?"

"Just the usual things." A repressed smile struggled to form. "I knew she hated licorice, loved the smell of cut grass, never saw Star Wars—"

"What?" Zach looked appalled, all bug eyes and whale mouth. "How can anyone never have—"

"What else, Mr. Meadows?"

"She liked to dance even though I have two left feet, she enjoyed going to the Lakewood Baptist Church, as a child she was attacked by a gerbil, she—"

"A gerbil attack?" Again, Zach channeled his inner wonder child. Zora planned on giving him a good spanking later. For now, an icy stare had to suffice.

Martin's pseudo-smile fell. Tears welled in his eyes. "It was a particularly nasty gerbil."

"There, there, Martin, let it out." The way Melora's hands roamed Martin's back, Zora wondered if she had some masseuse blood running through her icebox veins.

"Take your time, Mr. Meadows."

"That's all, really. Just the usual stuff a man knows about his wife. Until he doesn't know her."

Interesting. But not exactly what Zora'd been looking for. "Mr. Meadows...have you ever heard of Benito's Bandits?"

He dabbed at his eyes and straightened, the curtain dropping on his rare display of emotion. "Benito's...no, I'm afraid I haven't. Is it a Mexican restaurant? Tell me dear Misty wasn't also...working as a *waitress.*" On the edge of the seat, he appeared horrified at the notion.

"No, no, nothing like that. Don't mind me, I don't know where my head is today. Mr. Meadows, I know this is a sensitive question, but why do you think Misty kept her massage day-job a secret from you? It was a legit business concern and—"

"Hmph. Not in my world," said Melora.

Martin stared at Zora, blinkety-blinking. "Isn't it obvious, Ms. LeFevre?" *Not at all.* "She knew I wouldn't approve of that…life-style. It went against everything we believed in. Or I thought she believed in."

"How's that?"

Melora tossed her hands up. "Putting her hands on other filthy men and—"

"I'm not filthy," muttered Zach. Zora begged to differ but let it slide.

"It's as Melora says…her massage therapy was an act of intimacy. One only shared in a bedroom of betrothal."

Zora wanted to argue. Someone had to stand up for the late Mrs. Meadows. But she knew better than to preach. Especially when she needed to conserve her strength for one final salvo, the one she'd been dreading. "Um…I hate to ask this, but…where were you this morning and afternoon?"

"What?" Melora shot to her feet, straightening her long, frumpy skirt. "This is an outrage! You think you can barge in here, bothering my poor brother and then accuse him of—"

"I'm sorry, you misunderstand me. I'm not accusing Mr. Meadows of anything. As a client of mine, I want to protect him. Make sure he's covered in case the police suspect—"

"It's high time for you to leave!"

"Settle down, Melora. Ms. LeFevre's just doing her job. As every day except for Sunday, of course, as it's the Lord's Day…"

"Praise Him!" Obediently, Melora dropped to the couch, hands up. Mouth shut. *Thankyou God.*

"Praise Him, praise Him, praise Him," echoed Zora. "You were saying, Mr. Meadows?"

"Yes, I was at work. At my accounting firm, Delta and Niles. All day until the police called on me. At least fifteen people can vouch for me. The police have already corroborated this information."

"I have no doubt. It's just best for you to be prepared. Mr. Meadows, I'm going to find out who did this to your wife. I'll—"

"Can't you just leave well enough alone?" snapped Melora. "The damage is done. You're upsetting poor Martin again."

Martin, still in a hazy world of masseuse revelations, just shook his head, burrowing his gaze into the carpet. "You've done your job, Ms. LeFevre. You're relieved of your duties. I'll send a check soon."

Huh. Again, not the response Zora expected.

"Mr. Meadows, I won't expect you to pay me. Call it pro bono. I just want to see justice—"

"Zip it!" Melora, ever the literal librarian, pulled her fingers across her lips. "Respect Martin's wishes!"

"Of course, of course."

"Now...get out!" Melora jumped up, ankles snapping like broken twigs. With a harrumph, she wheeled. "Follow me."

"Just a moment, Melora." Martin stood, wiping his hands on the side of his slacks. "How'd she look? Misty?"

Oh boy. This can't be good.

"Mr. Meadows, I don't think—"

"No, sis, it's cool. I got this." Zach closed one eye, looked toward the ceiling as if searching for leaks. Only leak in the room was in his brain. "She looked...lovely. Very at peace. Almost as if...asleep."

Handled much more sensitively than Zora thought Zach capable.

Martin nodded, a crank lowering himself back into his sofa. "Good. Good." He sunk his head into his hands. "I still can't believe she was a...masseuse."

"Massage therapist," mumbled Zach.

"Get out," whispered Melora.

Zora grabbed her brother's wrist, pulling him behind before the Dragon Lady physically threw them out. Zora had no doubt she had the strength to do so.

At the door, Zora turned and said, "Again, I'm sorry about the intrusion, Miss Meadows. If I have any more questions, I hope you don't mind—"

Slam!

The door nearly missed her nose.

"I think that went pretty well, don't you, sis? Now can you drop me at the Bone-In Beef Club?"

As they climbed into the van, Melora Meadows opened the door again to watch them leave. Her fist rattled, her lips flapping. Zak imagined her screaming *"You kids get outta this investigation!"*

Scary.

"Sis, let's get out of here before Sister Melora brings down a plague of locusts."

Zora had the van backed into the street before her seatbelt clicked.

"Kinda prickly, wasn't she? Now stop yappin' and let me think."

He hated when his sister got in a mood. Time of the month, no doubt. But he'd long ago learned not to question her about it. Learned it in high school, as a matter of fact.

"Seriously, Sis, I dunno what else I can do, so if you just wanna drop me off at the Bone-In, I'll just—"

"Go to prison and latch onto some big thug's belt loop."

Like a home movie, snapshots of a desperately horrible future flashed through Zach's mind. "You don't really think I'm—"

"Call Dad. Find out where they are."

"Mom and Dad don't—"

"Have cell phones 'cause there's a government conspiracy to cause brain cancer. Yeah, I know. How could I forget? Call Nikki and put it on speaker."

"Right." Zach punched his screen.

On speaker phone, Nikki's voice banged out louder than the others. "Uncle Zach? *Where's Mommmmmmmmmm?* We *need* her!"

"Now, Nikki, we're doing just fine!" Sunshine's voice floated in that sing-songy tone of hers that someone, somewhere, thought was a great idea, even over Samantha's wails.

"Mom, do I need to call 911 or what?" Zora's eyes widened in alarm.

"Justin grabbed one of my tater tots! *So* unfair! Will you *please* come get us?"

"Where are you?"

"Sonic. Like you said. Duh."

"Nikki, there's more than one Sonic. And don't 'duh' your mother!"

"Grandpa? Where are we? *Hell?*"

"Nikki! Swear jar!" Zora'd never heard her oldest daughter curse before. Under the circumstances, she couldn't blame her.

"The one over in Merriam." Kelp shouted the location over the wails. "Samantha, pull Grandpa's finger!"

Zora rolled her eyes. "Samantha, do *not* pull Grandpa's finger! We'll be there in a few, Nikki, hang tough."

"So..." Thrilled that Zora's anger was diverted toward their parents, Zach asked what was really nagging him. "You like Martin for the death of his wife?"

"I don't 'like' anyone. 'Liking' is for high school kids with crushes. Quit watching TV cop shows!"

"But...they're, like, based on reality and—"

"I wonder what your world looks like, Zach."

Zach thought about it. Usually his world looked pretty spectacular. Super-stardom. Adoring fans. Meeting lots of ladies. Then he realized Zora wasn't *truly* asking about his world, just one of those weird things she does. "Okay, fine, whatever."

"Don't 'whatever' me! I get that enough from my kids!"

"Hey, white flag already! I just wanna clear my good name is all."

"What could *possibly* be good about the 'Banana Hammock Bandit' name?"

"You know what I mean. Besides, I still got a show to do tonight. Headliner and all."

"Zora to Zach, come in! Calling Zach...hellooo! Your freedom's at stake. And do you really have to wear your gross stripper pants everywhere you go?"

"They're male entertainment dancer pants. And like a scout, it's always best to be prepared. You never know when I might have to swing into action and take off my—"

"What's *wrong* with you? I know one of us is adopted, just know it."

"No way, sis. If that's the case, then we're both adopted. From the same biological parents. We love each other too much, think the same way. You know, blood's thicker than wine and all that."

Zora snorted, her go-to disguise for a laugh. "You got that right. 'Cause I sure as hell wouldn't be going through this if I didn't love you, idiot."

"I know, right?" Reinvigorated, Zach clapped his hands together and rubbed them. "So...do you think Martin did it?"

"Doubtful. I'm sure the police corroborated his alibi. Hard to get fifteen witnesses to lie, especially if you're a highly visible star accountant."

"Huh. What about the sister? She's scary enough to kill."

Zora tugged at her lip, her nervous habit when she thinks no one's watching. "I've thought about that. Actually, I wanted to ask where she was, but didn't get the chance. She bounced us out of there fast and I know from experience you don't question hostile people."

"I was kinda wondering why you didn't get her whereabouts."

"Okay, Detective Hasselhoff, you wanna take over the investigation?"

Of course Zach didn't. He had a show to perform. "No...no, no, no."

"Fine. Then let me detect. Melora doesn't really fit the bill. For killing, I mean. But, yeah...her alibi definitely needs to get checked out. I need more information before I jump all over her again, though."

"Hey, you keep bringing this up, what's the deal with Benito's Bandits, anyway?"

"Don't worry your pretty lil' head about it. But it might be our next stop. If I can figure out where to stop."

"You know I can't eat Mexican food, sis."

"Right. Because you're body's a temple and all."

Zach smiled and nodded. Making headway with his headstrong sister.

Mom and Dad's eyesore of a van stuck out like an ugly canker sore. Zora idled up next to it and killed the engine.

"Thanks, guys, for watching the kids."

Behind the wheel, Kelp leaned forward and hollered, "Hey, anything to help out our favorite ballet star son. Oh, and you too, Zora."

Zach soaked in the spotlight, his favorite spot. Couldn't help but notice Zora shaking her head, huffing up a fit. "Love you, too, Dad. It's so cool you guys support my art."

Justin leaned out the back window, a chocolate goatee framing his mouth. "Mommy, Mommy, we had Sonics!"

Next to him, Nikki rolled her eyes. "Gah! You're sooo way stupid! It's not plural!"

"You're prural!" Justin stumbled over the words. "And *you're* stupid!"

"I can't believe I'm even related to you! *Mommm!* Tell Justin he's adopted!"

"What's 'dropted'?"

"Quiet Nikki! Justin, you're not adopted." Zora drummed her fingers over the steering wheel, audibly counting to ten. Looking like she wanted to put all her kids up for adoption. "Mom, Dad, we might have another stop to make. Can you take the kids back to your place for a while?"

"Sure, no problem," said Sunshine. "It's groovy."

Justin cheered. Nikki groaned.

Kelp yelled, "Where ya goin'?"

"I need to check in with an old work friend of mine, find out about a group called Benito's Bandits."

"Oh. Oh, my," said Sunshine.

Kelp's eyes went wide. His hand slipped on the horn.

Bap!

From the back seat, Justin parroted the horn. *"Beep, beep, beep—"*

"Quiet, Justin! Dad…Mom…do you know something about Benito's Bandits?" *A long shot, but never discount my folks for craziness.*

"Jumpin' Jesus on a pogo-stick, I sure—"

"Grandpa!" Nikki thrust an open hand over Kelp's shoulder. "Swear jar!"

"Oh, right." Kelp chuckled, digging deep into his jeans pocket. Not too deep, though. He pulled out a nickel and slapped it into Nikki's greedy palm.

Nikki sat back, dramatically sighing. Zach felt for her. Kelp still thought the value of a nickel was worth…well, five cents.

"Dad! Stay focused! It's important. What can you tell me about Benito's Bandits?"

"Well, back in the day—"

"Dad! Can we not yell about this in the Sonic parking lot?" Zora unsnapped her seatbelt. "Honestly!"

Like old times, Zach plunged in behind his sister into the mysterious smelly confines of the love van.

Immediately, Zora took in a whiff, opened her mouth to breathe through it. "What have you guys been doing in here? Smells like a boy's locker room."

Kelp swiveled in his bucket seat. "Heh. Well, you know what they say about ol' habits and all. Sometimes your mom and I still like to—"

"Dad! Little ears!"

"Ain't nothin' wrong with a little good ol'-fashioned sex now and then."

"What's sex?" asked Justin. Of course Nikki rolled her eyes, a little too knowingly for Zora's tastes. Seven going on 21-year-old girl gone wild.

"Never mind, Justin. Big people are talking."

"I'm big, too!"

In a crouch, Zach searched for an uncluttered place to sit, stopping in front of Zora. "Dammit! Get your butt outta my face, Zach!"

"Mom!"

Already prepared, Zora tossed Nikki a quarter. Quite the up-'n'-coming entrepreneur, her daughter.

"Just looking for a place to sit."

"Move it!" She shoved Zach aside. He stumbled onto a worn mattress, legs up, pelvic bone again showing.

"Kids, kids," said Sunshine. "Am I gonna have to separate you two?"

"She started it," groused Zach.

"Oh, for pity's sake." Perched on the edge of her seat, Sunshine looked like she was ready to swat the two of them. "Look what kind of example you're setting for your children, Zora!"

"Me? What about Zach? He's the one thrusting his gross butt in my face. Something he's used to, by the way!"

"Why, I don't understand what in the world you mean, Zora," said Sunshine.

Zach scrambled to save his much-viewed butt. "You know Zora, Mom. That weird sense of humor of hers."

Justin watched the squabble with mild disinterest while Nikki filmed it with her phone.

"Nikki, you're *not* posting that," said Zora. "Anyway…Dad, what can you tell me about Benito's Bandits?"

"Well, your mom and I joined them in some of their rallies back in the day."

"What kind of rallies?"

"I dunno. Anything against 'The Man,' that sorta thing. I guess the Bandits were based on some old Mexican rebel or something." Kelp shrugged. "Never really understood that part. But we had fun for a while. Didn't really matter about the cause."

"Way to commit, Dad."

"Things were gettin' a little violent for our pacifistic tastes, though. Right, Sunshine?"

"That's right."

"So we quit. Why the interest in Benito's Bandits anyway?"

"Apparently the dead woman in question, Misty Meadows, had been a member of—"

"The lil' Saunders girl?" Kelp lifted his grey brows. "We knew her. Knew her folks, too. Bob and Angie Saunders!"

"They were Benito's Bandit members?"

"Sure were. Why, back in the day, we had some good times. Can't reckon I 'member 'em all, though. Why there was one time, we all ended up in a hot tub and—"

"Let's not go poking down memory lane. At least that dark alley. You're sure Misty's parents were members?"

"Sure as the hair on the back of my neck! Lil' Misty was born in the Rodriquez compound."

"Huh." So much for Misty's parents being farmers. Zora wondered what other secrets the late Mrs. Meadows may've been hiding. "They still active, Dad?"

"Don't know for sure. They're kinda in hiding. Carlos and Della. Think they're still wanted by the pigs."

"You know where they are? I think I'd like to have a little chat with them."

"Well…if they're still out at their farm, yeah. But, um…Zora you can't just walk up and knock on their door."

"Why not?"

"They're…a little paranoid. Best if Sunshine and I go with you."

The last thing Zora wanted to do was have her parents get in the way of her investigation. But for once, maybe their presence would be beneficial.

"Fine. Looks like a family outing."

Justin cheered. Nikki groaned. Zach looked clueless (no surprise there) while Zora wondered if she'd just made a colossal mistake.

Chapter Four

When Kelp pulled his van into the gravel driveway, a flurry of chickens squawked, running for cover. Zora parked behind him.

"Come on, kids. Stay close to me." Kelp's comments about the Rodriguezes' paranoid tendencies weren't exactly inspiring Zora's confidence.

"Chickens!" Justin hopped out, immediately chasing after the fowls with his arms out, a miniature Frankenstein monster.

"Justin! Get back here!" Too late. He'd already donned his selective-hearing helmet.

Kelp put his hand beside his mouth and stage-whispered to Zora, "Whatever you do, don't mention Carlos's eyes. Bad explosives accident."

"Wait…what?" The small house's screen door thwacked open, popping like a firecracker. "Hey! Hey! What're you doin' on my property?"

Ka-chak!

A shotgun barrel poked outside. "Gonna blast you to kingdom come!"

"Whoa! Hold on! Kids, get behind me!" Zora gathered her flock, using Theresa and her carrier to corral them behind her. Justin continued his chickenly pursuit, undeterred.

"Carlos! That you, man?" yelled Kelp. "It's me and Sunshine!"

Chik.

The barrel lowered. A thin man, dressed in a faded *Acid Is Groovy!* T-shirt, stepped out onto the porch. "Kelp? Well, I'll be hog-tied and battered! Ain't you a sight for sore eyes!" He ran off the porch, dangerously jogging with gun in fist. His free hand extended for a soul handshake to Kelp, apparently the international language of hippiedom.

"Good to see you, Carlos." The two old hippies exchanged pats and hugs, hands roaming everywhere. Carlos looked like he was covertly searching Kelp for a wire. They stood giggling at one another, a sort of geriatric, distaff version of the way the silly girls in high school used to do.

Then Carlos stopped, suddenly aware of Zora, Zach and the kids. His eyes narrowed, glaring at Zora. Or at least she thought he was glaring at her. Hard to tell. One eye wandered east, the other travelling west. "Wait a minute…who's this?" He fondled the gun, bringing it in closer.

"Ah, that's my kids, Zach and Zora. And Zora's herd."

"You vouch for 'em, Kelp?"

"That I do."

"Then your word's good." He softened again, heading straight for another love fest with Sunshine. "How you keepin' on, Sunshine?"

"Fine and dandy. You?"

"Can't complain."

Justin strolled up, out of breath. Jaw hanging open, staring at Carlos's meandering eyes.

Crap.

"Mister, what's wrong with your—"

Zora swooped in, hand clamped over Justin's mouth. "Chickens. Justin's never seen a live chicken before."

Carlos dropped, hands on knees, gun under his arm. He poked Justin's nose, a move all old people seemed to think children liked. Dumbfounded, Justin struggled beneath Zora's death-grip, mumbling.

"You like my chickens, do ya?"

Justin nodded. Zora released her captive, the danger passed.

"Shoulda been here last week, kiddo. We fried up one of the chickens good and right. First I grabbed its neck…" He curled a bony fist tight. "…then, got out my axe. *Thwack!*" His fist hit an open palm. "Took the head clean off."

Oh boy.

Justin's eyes grew wide, enthralled yet horrified.

"Mommmmmmmmmmmmmmmmmmmmm!"

Zora had a good idea what was coming, considered telling Carlos to shut up. Her investigation hinged upon gaining Carlos's trust, his loosening up, flapping his lips about Misty. Yet she didn't want Justin traumatized either. Then again, Justin was the devil boy who enjoyed lighting ants on fire beneath a magnifying glass. Strange kid would probably enjoy it. One to keep her eye on. Social experiment wins out.

"Then the damn body started chasing after me through the yard. Without its head! Heh. Never seen anything like it in all my days!" He chortled, a deep, raspy sound.

Didn't take a genius—or even Zach, for that matter—to know what came next. Three seconds to blast-off. Justin blinked, pondering the tale of the headless chicken. Then he drew in a huge breath, his chest expanding.

Zora had two choices: secure Justin's mouth again; or protect her own ears. Self-preservation won out. She covered her ears.

"Mommmmmmm!"

Torn between her job and her boy, Zora dropped her hands over Justin's shoulders, an anchor ready to end the freak-show.

"Heh. Boy-o, that old chicken ran around for several minutes without its head, blood gushing everywhere like a chocolate fountain!"

"I don't wanna eat chickennnnnnnnn!"

"Didn't drop for the longest time either, just kept on runnin' crazy, headless figure eights."

"Mommmmmm!"

"Just part of nature, son."

"Nooo—"

"Okay, Carlos, I think Justin's heard enough about chickens."

Carlos abruptly dropped his teasing-old-man persona. He cracked his wizened body taller, growled with nearly feral fury. His nostrils flared, eyes wide and bloodshot, his sudden rage aimed at Nikki. "*What* in the holy hell you think you're *doin'*, *girl*?"

Crap.

Zora's oldest child and biggest wise-ass held her phone, recording everything.

Time to run intervention.

Zora hustled to her daughter's side, pushing down her phone. "Nikki! Put that away now!"

Carlos tried to fix Nikki with his eyes but failed. "Just *who* are you, *really*? Why're you *filmin'* me?"

"Mr. Rodriguez, I assure you we're Kelp and Sunshine's children. My daughter meant no harm. She's just—"

"*Break* the phone!"

"What? *Mommmmmm, nooooo!*"

"Quiet, Nikki! It's just a hobby of hers, Carlos. I'll have her erase the footage and—"

"I mean it! Break the damn *phone*!"

"Nooooo!"

Kelp stepped forward, dropped a hand on Carlos's back. "Now, now, Carlos, the young 'un ain't no spy for the government. It's just the way kids are today. Tell you what, how 'bout she turns the phone off, puts it in the car? Takes the battery out?"

Carlos narrowed his eyes, paranoia churning. "I dunno."

"It'll be fine. Would I ever steer you wrong?"

Braaakkk!

A swirl of psychedelic colors burst from the slamming screen door, torpedoing through the yard. The stout woman, her tie-died sundress flowing behind her, didn't stop until she tossed her arms around Sunshine's neck, nearly taking them both down.

"Thought I recognized you, Sunshine! How're you?"

"Della! You look great!"

The two elder hippy women raised their screams into indecipherable gibberish, powerful enough to drown out the squawking chickens, Zora's screaming son and potentially stop the world on its axis. But it defused the time-bomb within Carlos. He joined the women in a group hug. So did Kelp.

"Um...this is all great and everything, but can we get down to business?" asked Zora.

Della broke away from the impromptu love-in. "And who might you be, missy?"

"That's my son over yonder, Zach," said Kelp, continuing to shove Zora to second-class. "He's a world-class, K.C. Ballet trained dancer. And that's my daughter, Zora, and her offspring."

"A baby!" Della ignored Zora and honed in on the baby cargo. "It's been years since we've had a baby on the farm!" She prodded a stubby finger at Theresa's chest. Frustrated, she did it again, trying to wake the baby up. Purely by instinct, Zora swung the carrier away. Never knew where that finger might've been.

"Sorry," said Zora, "Theresa can sleep through a tornado."

Della threw in the towel and turned her attention toward Justin.

"Well, look at you!" Della duck-walked toward Justin, fingers snapping like a lobster's pincers.

Justin sought cover behind his mother. "Mommy?"

"It's alright, honey." Zora stuck her hand out, hoped she wouldn't get pinched. "Pleased to meet you, Mrs. Rodriquez."

"Pshaw! None of that 'Mrs.' stuff here, young lady." She grappled with Zora's hand until she rearranged it into a soul handshake. "Come in, come in! I've got some herbal tea brewing."

The gaggle of hippies entered, practically frothing at the sound of tea, Zora supposed. Zach shrugged and went inside. Zora rounded up her crew, mentally counting them so as not to leave any unattended. Not for the first time, she thought a checklist might be convenient. She put keeping a written to-do checklist on the mental to-do checklist which she hoped to actually write someday.

Sitar music surrounded them, loud and irritating. Behind hanging beads, her father roared with laughter. She pulled the beads aside and stepped into a den of iniquity.

Faded posters from an even more faded decade hung on the walls. Beanbags lazily littered the room, slumping like forgotten, boneless dead men. Sunshine sat on the floor, cross-legged, closely facing Della. The two older men sat on a threadbare sofa in front of a coffee table buried under pot-smoking pipes and items Zora couldn't—or didn't want to—identify.

Justin picked up a bong and blew into it, imitating a dinosaur roar. "Look, Mommy, a saxy phone!"

Nikki, holding her elbows as if cold, rolled her eyes. "Gah! Sooo dumb! That's not a saxophone, dummy! It's a—"

"It's *not* a toy!" Zora snatched it away from her son and hid it behind her back.

Kelp finally snapped to attention and started moving the paraphernalia to a smaller table beside him.

All Zora could think about was how child welfare services would have a blast if they heard about the grand adventure she'd taken her children on today. Best to end this quickly. "I'm afraid this isn't a social call. I'm sorry to tell you that this morning Misty Meadows was found dead in a hotel room. You might've known her as Melissa Saunders."

Carlos blinked at her. Did it again, fluttering his lids like a kite in the wind. Finally, Della said, "Little Misty?"

"'Fraid so, Della. Can you, ah, tell me what you knew about the late Mrs. Meadows?"

"Whoa...whoa..." Carlos's eyes grew glassy and vacant, probably not so uncommon for him. He retreated into some other place, rocking, repeating his mantra of "whoa."

"How did this happen?" asked Della.

"We...don't know. But it's what I'm trying to find out. I need your help. Tell me about Misty."

"Wait...you're not one of them fascist pigs, are ya?" asked Della.

"No, no. She's in the..." Kelp sniffed. "...private sector. An investigator."

"Well, I'll be... Fine. If it helps find out what happened to little Misty, then we'll tell you all we can. Ain't that right, Carlos?"

"Whoa..."

Della, probably used to it, ignored her catatonic husband. "What do you want to know?"

"I understand Misty was born in your, ah, commune? Benito's Bandits?"

Carlos snapped to. "Wait...we don't know what you're talking about! We don't know nothin'!"

Kelp scooted over next to Carlos, pulled him into a shoulder to shoulder hug. "It's cool, it's cool. My daughter's cool. Nothing to worry about, Carlos. Just tell her the truth, man. All she cares about is finding out what happened to Misty. Nothin' to do with the Bandits."

Still not sold, Carlos settled into another funk.

"That's right," Della continued. "Misty was born on the ol' acreage we had out in California. Maybe late '70's, early '80's?"

"And her parents were part of the Bandits?"

"Yep. Bob and Angie Saunders. They were quite the rabble-rousers, I tell ya. Sheer hell-raisers!" Justin gasped, held out his hand. Della leaned over and laid five on him. "Not like little Misty."

"What do you mean?"

"Girl never really had the rebellion in her. Head in the clouds, that one, always dreaming. Putting on makeup, reading movie star magazines. Her parents pushed her, sometimes too hard, I think, to join our cause."

"And what exactly *was* your cause, Della?"

She looked at Zora with disbelieving eyes. "Why, fighting the man, of course!"

"Of course." Best not to go down that nebulous track. "Anyway, you were saying about Misty?"

"Yes. Well, she finally agreed to take part in one of our anti-nuke rallies. Don't know that she really wanted to. But she did it anyway. I'm afraid things got pretty ugly and—"

"Whoa...whoa..."

"...Misty was one of the casualties. Got herself arrested. But I'll say this for her...girl didn't rat us out. Didn't say a word."

"Did she participate in any violence?"

Della slashed a hand down. "Heavens no! She chained herself to the fast-food restaurant door until the police came and—"

"Why a fast-food joint?"

"Well...we couldn't get close to a nuclear plant. So we improvised, of course."

"Of course."

"Anyway, funny thing is...we never saw little Misty again. It's almost like she used her situation to escape, pursue a different path."

From the pieces Zora'd been putting together, it sounded like a very believable scenario.

"What happened to her?"

Della shrugged. "I think she did a little time in jail. Not much. She was nearly an adult. We tried to see her, but she wouldn't see us. Didn't even wanna talk to her own parents."

"Are they still living? Her parents?"

"That I couldn't really tell you, I'm afraid. Once the Reagan dark era ended, no one seemed to care about our form of rebellion any more. We sorta drifted apart, disbanded. Even if we're still wanted. But we joined society, Carlos even took up a job as a salesman for—"

"What? No, no, no..." Kelp hung his head in his hands, his dream bubble popped.

"Anyway, we sorta lost track of everyone from the Bandits, including Misty's folks."

"Huh. Anything else you can tell me about Misty?"

"Well, yeah...oddest thing. Her parents wouldn't give up on her. They kept trying to contact her. One day Angie asked me to go along with her, thinking I might have more pull with Misty. Well, I dyed up my hair good and black, put on some sunglasses, and off we went. Misty'd married. To some creepy guy. What was his name, Carlos?"

"Whoa..."

"Um, was it Martin Meadows?"

Della snapped her fingers. "That's it!"

"Why'd you think he was creepy?"

"Pretty intense dude. Bible thumper, I think. He wouldn't let us see his wife. Just tole us to go away, before he called the pigs. I guess Misty'd told him everything about the Bandits. Didn't come right out and say it, but he practically threatened to blackmail us like a greedy fascist."

"Huh."

Now things were *really* interesting. Either Martin Meadows had lied to Zora about not knowing what Benito's Bandits were or he'd forgotten about them. Which seemed very unlikely. Accountants don't forget things. Another visit to the grieving husband just got put on the docket. "Okay. Thank you very much for your time. I, ah, gotta get my kids home. Time for their naps." It wasn't really. Her kids would never dream of napping. But she wanted to make a hasty getaway before it turned into a full-on, smoke-filled, hippy reunion.

Her kids just stared at her, which didn't help one bit. Nikki shook her head in disgust while Justin looked puzzled, clearly having forgotten that nap was the secret code word.

Zora raised her voice. "Isn't that right, Justin? Time for a *nap*!" She turned her head so the Rodriguezes couldn't see her and gave her son a hard stare while tipping her head several times in an effort to remind him.

A light finally went on in her tow-headed boy's head. He tore off, raising his airplane arms and sounding the engine. He strafed by Carlos, tipped over a bong. "Nrrrrrrrr! I'm a jet-fighter! Takka-takka-takka—"

"Oh my, yes, then!" Della jumped to her feet. The woman could move. "Time for our company to go! Isn't that right, Carlos?"

"What…whoa…"

"Thank you for your help, I'll see myself and my kids out!" Zora gestured for Zach to help gather the beasts and shoved them out the door.

"Crap."

"What now?" asked Zach.

"Now I gotta go try and drag our parents outta there to watch the kids."

Mission accomplished, Zach and Zora climbed into Zora's van. Zach waved at the kids, standing in front of his parents by their van.

"Gah. I hate leaving my brat-pack with the older, worse pack."

"Geeze, sis, why not just bring the kids along?"

"Yeah, right. A murder investigation isn't a place for my kids. They do know Theresa's there, right?"

"Hand-delivered her to Mom myself."

"Yeah, but my baby's so quiet. God's gift. Wish the other ones would plug in to Heaven. But, you know, leave it to our folks to forget Theresa's even there."

"Relax, sis, they'll be fine. So…what'd you think of Carlos and Della? Killers?"

"Never discount anyone. Doubt it, though. Carlos looked pretty stunned by Mrs. Meadows's death. Plus…don't think he had enough synapses firing to pull off a smooth murder. I mean, did you see the guy?"

"Yeah. Didn't know if he ever saw me, though." Simultaneously, they both nodded, a sibling habit they'd perfected without ever practicing. Zach dusted off some of his own synapses, hoping he wouldn't end up like Carlos. "So…where to next?"

"Well, I think we need to have another chat with Mr. Meadows."

"Noooooo—"

"Clearly, he lied to us about Benito's Bandits. That makes me go *hmm*. But first I wanna make another stop."

"What? Where?"

"The Lakewood Baptist Church. Prepare to get some religion."

"Noooooo! *Why?*"

"Oh my God, you're worse than one of my kids! I want to find out more about Misty and Martin Meadows. And I don't think we're getting the full story from Martin and his sister."

"But I hate going to church! It's full of…scary people who look at me funny and—"

"Suck it up, already. What's your deal, anyway? You're afraid of seeing Mom and Dad. You—"

"Not afraid."

"…act like you're gonna burn in a church. But you take off your clothes in a revolting dive for everyone to see you naked!"

"Not a dive. And I don't take off *all* my clothes."

"Oh, how could I forget. You wear your precious disgusting banana hammock."

"Precious to me."

"Disgusting to me. Now get ready. We're here."

A big-ass church, not quite in the mega-category, stood tall in the sky blocking out God's rays of sunshine. Shadows draped over the massive front like a tarp. The sight terrified Zach. All glass walls and windows, the better to look into Zach's soul. He was sure the constituents wouldn't approve of his male entertainment dancing career. The cross at the top of the church pointed to Heaven, like a scary lightning rod. All very judgey.

For a Wednesday, quite a few cars sat in the newly paved lot. "Um, maybe I'll just sit in the car, Zor."

"Oh, no! I'm not doing all the work! Besides who knows what kinda trouble you'd get into on your own."

"Hey, I don't get into trouble! I—"

"Really, Zach? *Really?* Tell that to your dead masseuse."

"Massage therapist."

"Whatever! Let's go. I'll do the talking."

No way out of it, Zach hitched up his tear-away pants and followed Zora through the front doors. Cold air blasted him, the frigid temperature of judgment. From within the cathedral, a solemn organ tortured a dirge. It'd been years since Zach had entered a church. Quickly, he looked at his arm, checking to see if he'd burned. Never hurt to be careful. As an afterthought, he whipped out his pocket-sized moisturizer from his fanny pack, applying a thick coat to his face and arms.

"Stop it, Zach."

Zora found an OFFICE sign and followed the arrow. A middle-aged woman sat behind the front desk, tapping on her computer. Finally, she took off her cat-eyed glasses and dropped them onto a chain around her neck. Rose red lips pouted, not a sexy pout by any means. Terrible start.

"Yes? How may I help you?"

Zora whipped out her wallet, flashed a phony badge. "KCMO police, ma'am. We'd like a few words with the pastor."

"I see. May I ask what this is in regard to?" Her eyes swept over Zach, settling on his pants. Uncomfortable, Zach dug his hands into his sides, searching for pockets that weren't there.

Note to self: get tear-away pants with pockets.

"Police business. Now if you'd just let the pastor know we're here, I'd appreciate it," said Zora.

"It's Pastor Don Sparks."

"Okay, please let Pastor Sparks know we're here."

The woman pinched her face into a multi-wrinkled mess and squinted into her computer screen. "Do you have an appointment?"

"What? No, we're the police!"

"Pastor Sparks is a *very* important man. I'm afraid he's booked until—"

"Hey, now..." Zach leaned over the desk, glanced at her nameplate. "...Katherine. Pretty name for a pretty woman." Her pout tightened, oblivious to Zach's charms. "I understand the pastor's a busy man. So are we. If you'll just let him—"

"He's not *here*." Guardedly, she swept the items from the edge of the desk where Zach had been hovering closer to her. A few back-handed gestures forced Zach back. "How *many* times must I *tell* you the pastor's not *in*?"

"Once woulda been swell. You might've led with that. When will he be back?" Zora asked.

Behind them, the door opened. Another cold breeze froze Zach to his guilt-ridden soul. A short, rotund man in a white suit poured in. Sweat rolled down his temples, darkening the underarms of his suit. But it was his hair that fascinated Zach. Or fake hair. The wig looked like a black cat curled up on top of his head, ready to attack upon awakening.

"Katherine, it's hotter than Hades itself outside," he hollered in a speedy voice, the kind usually reserved for carnival barkers. "And who have we here?" His eyes twinkled with Godliness as he gave Zora, then Zach, a full-bodied once-over.

"It's the police, Pastor Sparks," said Katherine. "They'd like a word with you."

Sparks's eyebrows lifted. "Oh? Well, of course, of course! Always glad to help out local law enforcement! This way, this way!" He raced past them to an office in the back.

Before Zach and Zora entered his office, he'd already seated himself behind his desk. A speaker on the wall belted out the organ music Zach had heard coming from the cathedral. Behind Sparks, a photo of Jesus hung, staring at Zach with sad, mournful eyes, as if saying *I know what you really are*. Zach averted his gaze, instead focusing on Sparks's incredibly black, incredibly tall wig, a licorice pompadour.

"Now, let me ask you something, officers..." He waited, eyebrows raised to heavenly heights.

"Miller and Zabriskie," said Zora. "I'd like to ask—"

"Have you heard the word of our Savior, Jesus Christ?" Sparks folded his hands over his belly, rocking in his chair.

Reeet, creeet, reeet...

Zach wondered exactly which word Sparks referred to. So he went for them all. "Oh, yeah, of course! Read the Bible many times. One of my favorite books!"

Zora gaped at him.

"That's just terrific. It's always fine to see today's youth take an interest in the Lord's words. How 'bout you, Officer Miller?" Sparks turned his attention to Zora.

"Um...it's Detective Miller. And we—"

"Why, of course it is! May I ask what denomination you are, Detective?"

"Ah...work in progress?"

The chair stopped rocking. So did Sparks's million-dollar smile. "Oh. I see."

"Anyway, I'd like to ask you about two of your constituents. Martin and Misty—"

"The Meadowses!" He clapped his hands, startling Zach. For a moment he thought thunder had cracked open the skies above, lightning seeking out his male dancing soul. "Of course! Two of our favorite members! Been with us for years." He leaned forward, hand next to his mouth. "Very strong tithers." Then he drudged up his serious damnation face, all jowly frowns. "Tell me they're not in trouble."

Zora glimpsed at Zach briefly, back to Sparks. "Ah, no...they're not in any trouble. Just doing a little background check. What can you tell us about them?"

Sparks dropped a hand on a worn Bible, stroking the cover. Practically hypnotized, Zach watched the man's wig, wondering what kept it in place. *So furry, so big...*

"Not much to tell, really. As I said, they're two of our favorite flock. Never miss a Sunday sermon. They participate in extra-curricular activities and—"

"Like what?"

"Hmm. Oh, you know, fund-raisers, spreading the word, coffee get-togethers. The usual."

"How long have they been married?"

"That I couldn't rightly tell you, Detective. I believe they were married in a different church before they came to us here at Lakewood."

"And when was that?"

"I reckon..." His fingers rat-tat-tatted on the desktop. "...goin' on five, maybe six years now."

"And would you consider them...happy?"

Sparks leaned across his desk, fingers interlaced, fixing Zach with a piercingly serious glare. "Happy? Happy how? It's my job—and the Lord Jesus's, of course—to see to the happiness of my followers. 'Course they're happy! Say, what's this really all about?"

"Just routine, Pastor. Did you ever have the opportunity to talk with either Martin or Misty one on one? Did Misty seem...troubled?"

"No, no, no. They were very happily married if that's what you're gettin' at. Always holdin' hands, strollin' together. Greeting people after church. Smiles all around. Now see here, Detectives...it's my duty as a soldier of God to look after my flock. If there's some sort of trouble, then I'd like to—"

"No trouble." Zora glanced down, shaking her head. "Could I ask where you were this morning and early afternoon, Pastor?"

"What? Why, I was sitting right here, meeting my constituents over various matters 'til I took a late lunch break."

"When was that?"

"Just before I met with you. Oh, 3:00 or so. You can check with Katherine if you must. I'm beginning to feel a little uncomfortable with this line of questioning. What're you not telling me?"

"Nothing we're at liberty to say now, I'm afraid. Anything else you can think of about the Meadowses?"

His hands went up, open palming to God. "That's everything I can think of."

"Well, thank you for your time, Pastor."

"Why don't you two love-birds come by this Sunday? I think you'll—"

"*Love-birds?*" Zach's stomach roiled at the thought. "We're not love-birds! We're—"

Zora kicked his ankle. "Partners. Partners at work. Thanks for the offer, Pastor, but—"

"But, nonsense!" Sparks jumped to his feet, raced around the desk. He grabbed Zach's hand within his clammy grasp. "Ain't no 'buts' when it comes to salvation!"

"Ah…"

"Now. Why don't you pray with me? Pray to the Almighty and ask for forgiveness!" He released Zach's hand and raised his. "Come on now." With more than a few grunts and the desk acting as his crutch, he dropped to his knees and folded his hands.

"Um, we really gotta—"

"Dear God in Heaven, please forgive these…" Like a man in a deep trance, he ignored Zach's pleas, rattling on. Zach felt the collar on his t-shirt tightening. Jesus stared down from the painting, eyes no longer so mournful, but kinda angry. Zach looked away, staring deeply into Sparks's wig.

So tall, so soft, so inviting…

Zora sighed, worked her way to her knees. She jerked her head for Zach to follow.

The things I have to do for my sister.

Back in the van, Zora laughed. First good laugh she'd had all day.

"What's so funny?"

"You should've seen yourself, Zach! White as a sheet and more frightened than a gazelle at the end of a rifle!"

Zach sighed. "It's *not* funny! Guy gave me the serious creeps. Especially that wig."

"Yeah, that *was* impressive, right?"

"So another dead end. Why'd you ask him where he'd been? Surely you don't think he—"

"I've learned to suspect everyone. Real life isn't like your TV shows, Zach. Not everything ties together before a commercial break. But...his alibi seems pretty tight. Especially if his secretary Miss Uptight America vouches for him."

"But we didn't learn anything!" Zach crossed an ankle over his knee, pulled at the tennis shoe's flaking striping. "We're never gonna get anywhere."

"Yeah, well...maybe, maybe not. The alternative's rejoining your new lil' buddies in jail."

"No!"

"What I thought."

"What's your next big idea?"

"Time to re-visit Mr. Meadows. It's getting on 4:00. Phillip's gonna be home in a couple hours. Still need to get dinner ready."

"Phillip. Pfft. How is ol' stick up the wazoo doing these days?"

"Better if you'd ever pay for the damage to the car you borrowed."

"I'm working on it."

"Maybe you better strip a little harder then."

For once, her brother didn't try to correct her. It seemed some of the fight had gone out of him. Things did look pretty much like they were dead-ending. One thing she did know, though. There was more to the Meadowses than white picket fences and blissful life in suburbia.

Nothing had changed since their earlier visit to the Meadows home. Still two cars in the drive, one presumably Martin's, the other Melora's. But with dusk falling, the house looked dark, ominous almost. Not to mention the open front door.

Warning bells clanged, Zora's instincts firing red-hot ALERT signs.

Zora killed the headlights early, pulled to a stop in front of the house. Turned off the car, waiting and watching the house for signs of life.

"What's wrong?"

"Dunno. Something. Door's open, lights are off."

"Maybe Martin's napping. Been through a lot."

"Maybe." Zora reached over, chunked open the glove box. Grabbed her gun.

"Whoa, whoa, whoa! The hell, sis? You really think that's necessary?"

"Could be. You stayin' or comin'?"

Zach craned his head, a visible shudder coursing through his shoulders. "Um…maybe you'll need my help."

Zora did a quick eye-roll and held a finger to her lips. Quietly they exited the car. Zach shadowed her closely, stepping on her heels.

"Dammit, back off a bit," she whispered.

At the doorway, Zora gestured for Zach to stay put. She stepped inside, swiveled the gun left, then right. Just inside the doorway, she nearly tripped on something. Or *someone*. The person groaned. Craggy woman's voice. *Melora*.

Zora flipped on the foyer light. At her back, Zach spotted the woman on the floor.

"Eeeek!"

"Quiet," Zora hissed. "My daughters scream more manly than you do! See how Melora's doing."

Zora continued into the darkness, gun up. In the hallway, she stopped. Listened. Aurally gauging how many people were in the house. Silence. But sometimes silence could be deadly.

"Mr. Meadows?" she said in a low voice.

She swept by the living room they'd adjourned in earlier. Then made her way down the hallway. Stillness filled the back rooms, physically devoid of life. A funny sensation she'd experienced before.

She cleared two more bedrooms and a bathroom, touching as little as possible. Still she turned on the lights. It somehow made it feel safer if not actually safe, sorta like a child shutting his eyes against potential horrors hiding beneath the bed.

The final room. The door stood ajar. "Mr. Meadows?" She pushed the door open. A dark figure huddled on the bed. *Crap*. With a sigh, she flipped on the light.

Mr. Martin Meadows had now officially been reunited with his late wife. With a heart-shaped blood spot on the front of his shirt, a deadly valentine.

Chapter Five

Satisfied the house was empty except for herself, Zack and the dead and wounded bodies, Zora raced back through the house. With one arm around Melora's shoulders, Zach held her in a sitting up position.

Zora knelt beside Melora. "Miss Meadows? How're you? Are you hurt?"

"What happened?" She looked around, her head wobbly as if her neck couldn't do its job. There was a dried blood mustache beneath her nose. She rubbed the back of her head, brought back a handful of blood. "Someone hit me."

Zach turned away and gulped as loud as an underwater bubble popping. Guy had no stomach for this. Maybe he needed to quit stumbling across dead people.

"Someone? Who?"

Melora shook her head. "I…dunno. The doorbell rang. I answered it. Then…I was out. I think my nose is broken!"

"Let me look." Zora didn't really know what to look for. But she needed answers. Quick. Before the inevitable screaming started. "I don't think it's broken. But you probably need a medic to look at the wound on the back of your head. Did you get a look at the person who hit you?"

"No. As I said…I opened the door…then nothing."

"Did you hear anything?"

"No…wait…how's Martin? Martin!" She struggled to stand. Gently, Zora pushed her back down. "You need to stay there, Miss Meadows. You've had a serious blow to—"

"Martin! Where's Martin! Oh, my *Lord*, Martin!"

For an older woman, she had some fight in her. No lightweight herself, Zora tried to counterweight her to the floor. Melora tossed her arms up, cutting an arc around her. A stray fist found Zora's cheek, knocking her back.

"Dammit! Zach, call an ambulance!"

Melora batted Zach away and crawled to her feet. Straightened out her long dress. Then took off for the back rooms, screaming, "Martin, Martin, Martin…"

That could've gone better.

A crescendo of a shriek erupted. Melora'd found her brother.

Against her better judgment, Zora called Soundtrack Saul. He groused and griped, put out by another murder. Probably got him off his bar stool.

The screaming wouldn't stop, more insistent than a fire engine's siren. Zora felt a mega-headache coming on. "Zach, go see if you can comfort Melora."

"Comfort her? Why?"

"You'll see."

Again, Zach's scream reached even higher heights than Melora's but at least Zora'd successfully banished the banshees to the back room. She needed to work fast and unimpeded.

She found gloves beneath the sink and quickly searched the house. Not as thoroughly as she'd like, but time was short. Ten minutes in she'd found absolutely nothing, just the signs of a life lived boring. Sounded kinda nice. When she heard Saul bellowing from the front door, she stripped off her gloves.

"Zora?"

"In here, Saul."

Saul, hitching up his ever-falling pants, huffed into the kitchen, followed by a uniformed officer. "You gotta be kidding me, right? Now Martin Meadows is dead?"

"As a doornail. Whatever that means."

"And you guys just happened to find the body again."

"What can I say, Saul? Luck be a lady tonight." As soon as she'd said it, she wanted to reclaim her words. She'd just handed Soundtrack

Saul his next happening hit, number one straight to the top with a bullet!

"Hm....hmmm, *hmmm, hmmmm, Ka-pow!*" Saul twirled, long enough for Zora to get a good eye-roll in. *"Luck be a lady tonighttttt! Zora, tell me we're not gonna have a fighttttt! Yeah! Unlucky for you and your stripper crewwww! You keep steppin' in the grueeeee!"*

Good grief, I'd rather be praying.

"Hey, that's pretty good, Saul!" Zora applauded, hoping to end the performance before he took a curtain call. "Here's what I—"

"Where's your stripper brother?" Out of breath, Saul pulled his pants up again. Really needed a tighter belt if he wanted to pursue the "arts."

"Zach? He's in the back with the corpse. And the sister."

His eyebrows lifted. "What? You think that's a good idea? 'Specially since he's my number one suspect?" He hurried down the hallway with Zora dogging him.

"Oh, hell, Saul. He's not your suspect. He's been with me all friggin' day."

"We'll just see 'bout that."

If Zach wasn't the number one suspect, he probably was now. Unbelievably he had Melora sprawled out on the bed next to her dead brother while he sat next to her, cradling her shoulders.

"What the holy *hell*? Get *off* the damn bed, stripper-boy!" yelled Saul.

"Not a stripper." Zach jumped off.

"Ma'am, there's an ambulance coming to give you a look-over," said Saul to Melora. "And, ah, one for your brother, as well."

Melora loosened the floodgates again. At least that wouldn't allow for a lot of singing from Saul tonight. He turned to the cop behind him. "Officer, please escort the poor woman out of the room."

The officer, looking only slightly less freaked out than Zach, coaxed Melora off the bed and led her away.

"That's Martin's sister," said Zora.

"Yeah, we met earlier. As I understand you did too, Zora. You're meddling again."

"Just doing my job."

"Right, right. Tell me everything."

"It's not much..." And it took less than a minute.

"That's it? The big picture? The entire enchilada?" As if struck by inspiration, Saul's eyes lit up, big old Broadway lights. *"The entire enchilada! Cha-cha! The—"*

"Saul! What about the body?"

"You touch it?"

"No." Under her voice, she added, "Can't say what my brother did, though."

"What's that?"

"Nothing. Looks like a bullet wound to the chest, yeah?"

On one foot, lifting the other behind him—a geriatric, balletic warm-up move—Saul leaned over, grimly nodded. "Looks that way. But I'm not the coroner."

"Neither am I. But it doesn't take a medical examiner to make that conclusion. Find out anything yet about how his wife died?"

Saul shrugged. "M.E.'s made some prelim exams, tossed around a couple thoughts, but nothing concrete yet."

"What's he got?"

"You know I can't tell you—"

"Saul! Dammit, we've been through this! Got my kids out in the car. If you want I'll bring 'em in so we can—". She didn't, of course, but Saul probably hadn't looked.

"No, no, no!" Saul tossed out defensive jazz hands. "They're thinking asphyxiation. No ligatures, though. Maybe from a pillow. And they found something on her neck. Tiny pin-point. Maybe some kinda drug to knock her out before her murder."

"Huh."

"Mean anything to you, Zora?"

"No. Just interesting. Two completely different M.O.s"

"Wouldn't be the first time. Okay, *quid pro quo*. What've you got?"

"Nothing, really. But I don't think Martin and Misty were the preciously married couple everyone thought they were."

"Oh, really? Tell me more."

"Mostly just a hunch. Everyone says how nice they were, but...Misty was clearly keeping secrets from her husband."

"Kinda what I'm finding out."

"First, her being a masseuse...then her past with Benito's Bandits."

Saul turned on her, hands digging for gold in his pockets. "Oh? And how'd you come by that info?"

"Oh, I dunno, Saul. Just lucky, I guess. What I said...luck be a lady!" *Take it away!*

"Luck be a lady tonighttttt! Luck be a lady tonighttt—"

"Yeah, um, I gotta go, Saul, if you're done with us."

Undeterred, Saul broke into the second song of his medley. *"Don't leave town, this hellava townnnnnn! I'll track you downnnnnn and—"*

"Bye, Saul. Keep up the great work!"

"Zora...oh, my God. This is bad."

"Bad, Zach? *That's* how you'd define this?"

"Really, really bad?"

"Eloquent."

"Thanks. Do the cops think I did it?"

"Think you're off the hook for this one. I can vouch for you. Maybe not so much the first murder."

"Why does this keep *happening* to me?"

"Because you're a stripper. *Duh.*"

"Male entertainment dancer. And it had nothing to do with that! *Duh.*"

"Don't you *duh* me, Zach! You're the definition of *duh*! Everything you do is *duh*!"

"You started it." Then he whispered, "Duh."

Ordinarily, Zora wouldn't have let Zach get the last word in. Not the way she rolled. But as they eased into the tail end of the rush-hour traffic on Metcalf Avenue, her rear-view mirror held her attention.

"Um, what's wrong, sis?"

"Quiet." Someone following them. She couldn't see the make of the car, only that it was old, not in great shape. A car that had been following them since they'd left the Meadows house. "Hang on."

She whipped over into the left lane, cutting off another car. An angry voice flared beside a horn burst. The mystery car shadowed her move.

"Dammit! Give me some warning next time, Zor!"

"Don't wet your tear-away pants, but we're being followed."

"What? Crap…not again. Followed by who?" Zach turned around, peering into the falling darkness.

"Don't look! And like I know who's following us! Maybe the killer. *Duh.*"

"The killer?" I'm too *young* to die! Is it a cop? I'm too *pretty* to go to—"

"Would you please just shut up!" Frustrated, Zora pulled up behind the long line of stalled cars, impatient workers striving to get home. Not going anywhere. The oncoming two lanes were moving at a slightly faster clip, still not the usual high speed for Metcalf during off-hours. In the distance, she spotted a cab, slowly working its way toward them. "Okay, get ready."

"*Ready?* Ready for *what*?"

"When I say go, go!"

"What do you *mean* by *go*?"

"Go!" Her gun tucked in her purse, Zora grabbed the keys from the ignition and exited.

"*Wait!* What the *hell're* you—"

"Follow me!" she called back.

Zora raced into the oncoming lane on foot, flagging down the approaching cab. Horns honked. Fists shook out windows. Curse words were hurled that would make her daughter rich. Three feet in front of her, the cab stopped with a screech. The driver's hands went up in an *are-you-crazy* gesture. Zora wrenched open the door and hopped in. Zach followed, flustered and hyper-ventilating.

"Lady, *what* do you think you're *doin'*?" asked the cab driver.

"Paying you to take us outta here."

The cabbie looked at Zach, then a smile dawned over his face. "Hey…you're that EZ Brite guy, right?"

Zach nodded. And flashed his stupid EZ Brite smile. "Yeah, hey, long time, man." He shook hands with the cabbie.

"Gah. *Please* tell me this isn't the same cabbie—"

"Sure is. Same cabbie who helped me out when I found my first dead body."

Zora groaned. "Just great. A reunion."

"Alright, for you, my friend, anything…where to?"

"Zach, give him your address."

"What? Why?"

"Just do it!"

As they pulled by the car that had been following them, Zora looked out the window. Several continent shaped splotches of bird droppings obscured her view. Zach leaned over and waved.

Zora slugged his shoulder. "Don't wave at the bad guys!"

The cabbie pushed down his flag. Cleared his throat. "You ready, guy? *EZ Brite makes your teeth white! EZ Brite gets the fight right! EZ Brite…*"

Zach joined him. And they didn't shut up until they reached Zach's apartment.

Zach shook the cabbie's hand again and scooted out after his sister. "Sis, you better pay Bennie."

She groaned. "Why in hell do I gotta pay him? I did it last time! And it's your mess!"

Zach shrugged. "Kinda low on cash this week."

"Shocker. Okay, anything to make you guys quit singing that damn song."

"Take care, Bennie!" Zach yelled as the cab took off.

"I swear, Zach…"

"What?" They walked up the sidewalk to his apartment. "I didn't do anything!"

She wheeled on him. "That's your problem!" A finger thumped his chest. "You never think you've done anything! This is the *second* time you've wound up as a murder suspect and still you walk around practically *singing* about how you haven't done anything!"

"Haven't been singing."

"No, just the EZ Brite song for about a zillion times! It's time you took some *responsibility* for your actions! What? You think I *wanted* to abandon my van on Metcalf to be impounded? You think Phillip's gonna be happy about *that?* And that there's no *dinner*... Oh crap. Phillip! I gotta call him!"

Zach fished out his keys, quickly slid one into his door. At the last moment, he regretted the decision. Zora'd never been to his apartment. And he hadn't had a chance to clean. But he sure didn't want her to keep yelling at him for the whole neighborhood to hear.

"Sorry about the mess, Zora. Wasn't exactly expecting company." He turned on the light.

As expected, Zora didn't respond well. "Oh...my...Gawd! You live in this...this squalor?" She toed a yawning pizza box at her feet. A slice of pepperoni flipped out onto her shoe. "Seriously?"

"Um...hey, the maid hasn't been by yet," he said with a grin.

"What the hell is all this?"

Granted, the apartment wasn't ready for *Better Homes and Gardens*, but it'd seen worse days. Fast-food bags and wrappers lay strewn about, just the way the man-on-the-go lives in modern society.

"I thought you didn't *pollute your temple* with fast food!"

Busted. "I usually don't. But, hey, I'm a busy guy, always running here and there. Gotta keep my strength up, sometimes with a quick dose of protein."

"Uh-huh. Right. You're also a 'male entertainment dancer.'"

"Finally!"

"Oh, whatever." Frazzled, she tossed her hands up and dug into her purse. "I gotta call Phillip. Just keep quiet. And put on some *real* grown-up pants!"

Zach escaped to his room. Unfortunately, laundry day hadn't rolled around yet this week. Or for the last couple of weeks. He kicked up another pair of tear-away paints, his second favorite. They didn't smell too bad. Maybe Zora wouldn't notice. Getting dark outside anyway.

Zora's voice drifted in from the bedroom. "Yes, I know, Phillip... I'm going to be late again... No, I won't be there for dinner... What? Try reading a recipe! Follow the instructions! Go buy a TV dinner! Go to Taco Fred's!... Too bad, so sad! I have a job too, you know... Oh, don't you *even* go there! Don't you *even* dare!... Your *job's* no more important... What? Yes, it's Zach again!... Because he's my brother, dammit!... That's what family does!... The kids? With my parents... You're gonna have to pick them up after you get off work... Hey, the day you hire a babysitter, let me know how that goes for you! The kids already broke all the ones I found!... Oh and by the way, the van's parked on Metcalf and is probably gonna be impounded. Bye, Phillip!"

She was steaming when Zach came out of his bedroom. "That man! I could strangle him!" Zach didn't doubt it, but he'd had more than his fair share of dead people for one day.

"Please, no! No more dead bodies today. And sis? Thanks. For everything you do for me. Really. You know I've always got your back too, even if it doesn't seem like it. You're my sister. I love you. That's what family does." He hugged her, usually the way to her heart. Every word he spoke was true. Plus it kept her slapping hands pinned.

"I know." She hugged back and then broke away. "Okay, enough sister-brother bonding. We gotta go." She slapped him on the shoulder.

"How? You left your van. And Bennie's gone."

"We're taking your car. It still runs right?"

"My Celica! It's still at the motel where Misty died!"

"Not talking about that. You still got your Trans Am, right?"

Crap. "Um, kinda."

"Kinda? Kinda? How do you kinda have a car? That's like saying there was sorta a tornado!"

"It's...got issues." His 1980 Pontiac Trans Am Turbo. His first car and his first love. He never could bring himself to sell it, a betrayal of sorts. Even though it barely ran. Still they say you never get over your first love. "Zor...it's not reliable." It wasn't. But, truthfully, he couldn't stand the thought of harm coming to it either. And there was the matter of the ankle high pile of fast-food wrappers decorating the floorboards.

"I abandoned my van! The least you can do is dust off your stupid hot rod!"

"Fine, sis, you win. But I might have to get gas."

"Gah. Still like a high school kid. Fine. We need wheels. Sucky as your car is."

"Not sucky! Ol' Becky was the coolest, bitchinest ride at Shawnee Mission North. She—"

"Okay, first of all, you know how dumb it is to name your car? Sexist, too. Why can't it be a 'Harvey' or a 'Donald'? Second, clearly you don't remember the car as it really was. You thought you had a souped-up hot rod. Instead, the thing barely kept up a fat man's jog. So embarrassing."

"You're the one not remembering things right! Becky always—"

"Quiet. Let me think."

In a hushed voice, Zach said, "was too a bitchin' car."

Zora plucked her lip, paced the floor. "Is there anything else you know about Misty? What about her other customers?"

"Well…yeah…Freddie goes to her. Or he did."

Zora stopped, eyes wide and firing on all cylinders. "You mean, 'Fireman Freddie'? From the strip club?"

"Yeah. And it's not a strip—"

Smak!

"Ow!"

"And you didn't think to tell me this earlier! What *else* did you forget to tell me?"

"Um, nothing…just that he told me about her in the first—"

Swat!

"Dammit! Enough! That's everything, I swear!"

"So your little friend—"

"Not my friend. We're frenemies!"

"Whatever! Let's go talk to your little play pal. Where is he?"

"At the Bone-In Beef Club. Where I should be right about now."

She groaned. "The things I go through for you."

"But I appreciate it, sis, really…truly."

"Let's go. Before I change my mind."

When he opened the door, Zach couldn't believe the girly shriek that filled his ears. Especially since it was his. But at the moment, he felt no shame. Because he stared into the dark tunnel of a gun barrel and hoped he wouldn't wet his tear-away pants.

"Back slowly into the apartment," whispered the masked gunman. Whisper or no whisper, the identity of the culprit was clearly evident to Zora.

"Do as he says, Zach." Zora took several steps back, just enough room for the gunman to enter.

Zach, three shades of bone-white, complied. Then the color flushed back into his face along with obvious relief. "Hey, man, what's goin' on? Why're you pointing a gun at us?"

"Shut up! I'm here to give you a warning. Leave the—"

"Why're you wearing a Bob Hope mask?" Zach dropped his hands.

"Zach, don't antagonize a man with a gun!" said Zora. "And it's Nixon, idiot, not Bob Hope!"

"No, I'm pretty sure you're wrong, Zor. It's definitely—"

"It's Richard Nixon, dammit!" As if unsure of his disguise, the gunman touched the hound-dog nose, straightened the rubber mask to better peer through the eye holes. "Now I'm gonna give you one warning, and one warning only, stay away from—"

"Oh, for God's sake, Carlos!" Indignantly, Zora thwacked her arms to her sides, tired of holding them up. "What in hell do you think you're doing?"

The gunman stuttered, found his vocal footing. "Carlos? I don't know any—"

"We know it's you! You're wearing the same *Acid is Groovy!* T-shirt you had on earlier today!"

"Crap. Um, I'm not Carlos. Just dig where I'm comin' from for a minute. Drop your investigation into Misty Meadows's death. You don't know what you're up against. You..." Again, he stuttered. This time not over his patter. Zach captured his attention, hypnotizing him like a snake charmer. "What're you doing?"

Zora knew. Incredibly dangerous and stupid when faced with a loaded gun. "Zach! *Don't!*"

Zach's "zone" moves. His left foot shuffled to the side, then the right. Back and forth, speed building. His fists drew up, his head craned at odd, practiced angles like an ancient Egyptian dancer. Shoulders, arms and fists warmed up to his legs. He feigned a few false jabs, ducked several times, while tossing out "hups" and "look outs!"

"Tell your brother to stop it!" Carlos backed up, flung a protective arm over his mask.

A fist jabbed into Nixon's rubber chin. Carlos flailed back, arms up like a rabid football fan. The door kept him upright. Zach twirled, brought a foot up into Carlos's stomach. Carlos dropped. The gun flipped out of his hand and fell into an open fast-food sack.

"*Yeah*, baby! *That's* what I'm talkin' about!" Zach lifted a foot to below his knee, took a celebratory spin. When he stopped, he placed a hand on the wall, dizzy. "Wow…must be out of shape." Then he reached for the gun.

"Stop! Don't touch the gun, Zach!" Zora nudged him away, then snatched the sack. "Carlos, why'd you shoot Martin Meadows?"

"What? Misty's husband? I didn't…hang on…" He wrestled the mask off. His long silver hair splayed out over his shoulders. "I didn't shoot Misty's husband. He's dead?"

"As doornails. Can *someone* please tell me what that means, already? Anyway, since you came at us with a gun, looks like you're the number one suspect."

"No! You gotta believe me! I didn't kill him!" Carlos tucked his legs beneath him, attempting to climb up.

"Stay down!" Zach bounced on his feet again, fists up. "Unless you want more of this."

"Okay, okay, fine. Jesus. I'm a pacifist!" Carlos slumped back against the door.

"Yeah, some pacifist." Zora rattled the bag. "Pacifists don't try to shoot people. And your record with Benito's Bandits speaks for itself."

"You got me all wrong. I wouldn't hurt Kelp and Sunshine's kids. The gun ain't even loaded. Check it if you don't believe me."

Zora peeked into the bag, took a whiff, testing for burnt cordite. Nothing but rancid fast food. "Zach, bring me some rubber or plastic gloves."

"What? I don't have any gloves like that! Why would I have—"

"Oh, for God's sake. Never mind." She pulled up a discarded wife-beater. When she tried to shake it out, parts remained stiff as cardboard. "What've you been using this for? Toilet paper?"

"Hey, it's my workout shirt."

"I don't even wanna know what a workout constitutes for you." She grabbed the soft part of the shirt, finagled the gun loosely into it and opened the chamber. Empty. She held it up to her nose. No odor other than a tangy old metal smell. "Fine, maybe you didn't use this gun. Maybe you used another. Where were you the past couple of hours?"

"Well, when you left, Kelp and Sunshine and your lil' ones stuck around for a while so we could catch up."

Now Zora was really pissed. Held at gunpoint was one thing, but her kids hanging out at an aging hippy party hadn't been on the babysitting agenda. Priorities, though. "How long did they stay?"

"Up 'til about a half hour or so ago. Them little ones of yours are quite a handful. Heh. Why they—"

"Then you came directly here? Why?"

"Guess I just got worried. About Benito's Bandits and all. You know we're kinda still wanted. I tossed it around with Della. She thought maybe I should just go talk to you. Ask if you could keep us out of it. But...old habits die hard. I found my Nixon mask next to my old gun—hadn't fired it in years, mind you—and those old feelings just started coming back. Thought I could kick-start a little bit of juice in the old sex life, you know. Why, whenever Della and I used to pull one of our protests, we'd—"

"Yeah, save it for Dr. Phil. You still came at us with a gun and—"

"An unloaded gun."

"Whatever. So...you thought you'd get us to back off?"

"Hopin' too, yeah."

"How'd you find us? At Zach's apartment?"

Carlos clicked the side of his mouth. "Well, Kelp told us where young Zach lived. Told us everything about him. How proud he is of his KC Ballet dancing—"

"Of course he did." Zora sighed, shook her head at the unjust caste system of siblings. "And you couldn't have just tried talking to us?"

"As I said...I felt the old burn, that jazzy feeling—"

"I know that feeling, sis."

"Shut up, Zach! For cryin' out loud, Carlos! We haven't mentioned you to the cops. Didn't plan on it either. Until now."

"Please don't do that. They'll put me and Della in prison. And she and the farm are all I got. Please, please, please don't—"

"Were you following us earlier? Down Metcalf?"

Puzzlement crinkled his face like an over-laundered shirt. "What? 'Course not! I came straight here!"

"What about Misty? You kill her?"

His eyes went wide. "Hell, no! Loved that girl like she was my own. And, um…you know, she just mighta been, too. Hard to say with all the lovin' that was goin' on back in the day."

Huh. And ewwwwwww.

"Carlos, I'd really rather not rehash your sex life. So if you didn't kill Misty…how 'bout you tell us who you think did."

A giant, worthless shrug. "My money woulda been on her husband. He was way over-protective of her, you know? Creepy dude."

"Creepy *dead* dude."

"Yeah, well there is that."

"What do you think we should do with him, Zach?" She really didn't give two hoots and a holler about Zach's opinion, but she needed someone to play "good cop" to her "bad cop."

"I dunno, sis… I kinda get where he's coming from. Sounds like he's been…what's the word…prostated, that's it. Yeah, he's been prostated a lot for his past."

"What the hell're you talking about, Zach? He's had a lot of prostate cancer?"

"Actually, I have!" Hope lit up Carlos's eyes.

"Be a good criminal, Carlos, and speak only when spoken to."

"Not a criminal. Well, not anymore, at least."

"And Zach," continued Zora, "if you're talking about being 'persecuted,' I really don't see him that way either."

"We hung up our old ways, Zora," said Carlos. "We're just two old folks who're trying to live out our days in peace."

"With guns. Bombs, too?"

"No." His shoulders slumped. Zora couldn't tell if it was out of defeat or nostalgia for the good ol' days. "We're just farmers now."

Crap. Odds were Carlos was telling the truth and she'd be wasting valuable time bringing in the cops and giving the killer more time. Besides, he reminded her of Kelp. Only one thing to do.

"Carlos…I'm gonna give you a little bit of time while I keep looking into who killed the Meadowses If it turns out you're telling the truth and—"

"I am! Call your parents!"

"Oh, I plan on doing that." For more reasons than establishing Carlos's alibi. "Anyway, if I find the killer—and it's not you—I don't see the need to give you and Della up as America's Most Wanted."

His eyes roved in every direction. "Oh, man, thanks! That's so damn groovy of—"

"Don't thank me yet, Carlos. You're not gonna like the next part."

"What're you talkin' about? Wait…*what*—"

"Zach?"

"Yeah?"

"Put his lights out."

For once, Zach followed her order without question. Even had a little smile on his face as he started his infernal dance prep.

"Nighty night, Carlos," said Zora as Carlos entered an enforced slumber land.

Chapter Six

"Why you had handcuffs—fur-lined ones!—I don't even wanna know!"

"See, sometimes I'm called in to for bachelorette parties. Make a little side dough." He rubbed out some imaginary Benjamins between his fingers. "And the girls seem to like the whole cop thing. They—"

"Enough!" Her hand leapt off the steering wheel, held out to Zach like a crossing guard. "Live out your juvenile, stunted fantasies on your own time."

"They're not stunted."

"You've been emotionally stunted since sixth grade. You're sure you tied up Carlos so he can't escape?"

"Yeah, just like you said."

"And you checked him for a cell phone?"

"Um, yeah." *No.*

She looked at him. "Whaddaya mean *um, yeah*? It's either yes or no! No *ums*!"

"Sure, yeah, of course! Have I ever let you down, sis?"

"You're not really asking me that, are you?"

"Um, yeah."

"Stop saying *um*!"

In the Bone-In Beef Club's parking lot, she jerked the car to a stop. "We're here. And I *hate* going into this sexist sleaze pit!"

"Hey, it's not sexist! We cater to women and gay men. Why we—"

"You don't even know what sexist means. Just get in the club, talk to your friend, Fireman Freddie—"

"Frenemy, not friend!"

"...and get out. And so help me, if you do anything embarrassing, I'll leave your ass here high and dry."

"We're in, um, my car."

"But it's my life!" When she slammed the door, the Trans Am shook like it had a high fever. Zach gave Becky a tender pat, whispered, "It's alright, girl." He ran to catch up to Zora joining the waiting line of ladies.

"Let me take it from here, sis." Zach nodded confidently, eyes closed, comfortable on his turf. His Kingdom. He strolled past the women to the head of the line.

"What's up?" he asked the doorman.

"Zach. You're in trouble. Missed your headlining spot. Evans is pretty pissed."

"Yeah, couldn't be helped. He here tonight? Evans?"

"Nope. You lucked out." The doorman peered around Zach. "Who's the pretty little lady?"

Zora shoved Zach aside. "A lady tough enough to kick your ass if you call me that again."

The doorman laughed and lifted the entry rope.

Home, sweet home!

The strobe lights blinked within the dark interior, bouncing to the beat of a power anthem vibrating the speakers. Adoring fans sat at tables, screaming and waving folded bills. Barely clad waiters, some of them doubling as dancers, skirted between tables, bussing trays full of drinks. The world's fattest dancer, Burly Brian, mercifully sat behind the DJ booth, announcing the dancers. Better he stay there then expose his flab to the world and turn the audience into salt. Happy to be home, Zach temporarily forgot about his predicament. At least, he was happy until he saw what was happening onstage. In the headlining spot. *Zach's* headlining spot.

Fireman Freddie, ridiculous in his fireman hat and yellow skin-tight pants, was waving around a fire hose. He pulled it through his legs, wiggling it in a grotesquely phallic manner. Absolutely no class.

Zach couldn't believe Evans had given Freddie his spot.

His world imploded, the day's horrors rushing back over him like a tidal wave over a sandcastle.

Zach turned to the bar, waved Shelley over. At least he didn't have to deal with Hairy Alan tonight, that would've been just one indignity too many.

"Shelly," he yelled, "why's Freddie headlining?"

With glass in one hand, towel in the other, she shrugged. "You didn't show, Zach. Hope you still have a job."

Crappity-crap-crap!

A fire alarm whined, signifying the end of Freddie's agonizing set. Freddie whipped off his yellow, plastic pants and tossed them over his shoulder. *Plastic, for crying out loud!* Before he exited, he walked the stage, strutting like an arrogant peacock. Clueless women stuffed bills into his G-string. Then he vanished through the curtains.

Zach turned and yelled over to Zora. "Sis, I'm goin' backstage to talk to Freddie."

"You're not going without me, dammit!"

"Sorry, sis, no women allowed backstage. Just make yourself comfy. I'll be right back."

"Wait! Dammit, Zach, how am I supposed to get comfy in…"

The music drowned out Zora's voice as Zach shouldered his way backstage. He found Freddie preening in front of a mirror, flexing a pathetically tiny bicep.

"Filmore!" said Zach. "I need to talk to you!"

Freddie turned, sneered. His baby mustache nearly vanished beneath his upturned lip. "Caulfield. What're *you* doin' here? Evans gave me the top spot tonight. Too bad, so sad. You didn't show. The price of show-biz."

"You call what you were doing out there show-biz? Don't make me laugh!" Zach couldn't help but puff out his chest a bit. Freddie always brought it out in him. "That was penny-ante, sidewalk, miming at best."

"Oh, yeah?" Freddie approached him. Fast. Their chests bumped, Freddie's slick with sweat and tons of oil. "I could out-dance you any day, anywhere, Caulfield!"

"Like to see you try it!" To establish domination, Zach leaned in, laid his forehead against Freddie's. Freddie's eyes melted into one cyclopean orb. Which actually suited his unibrow.

"I think you're afraid of me, Caulfield. That's what I think!" Freddie circled and Zach followed in their tango of hate.

"Sounds like a challenge to me, Fillmore! You're on!" Zach pumped a fist in the air. "Dance-off!"

"You got it! My jam, though!"

Oh, crap. That put Zach at a disadvantage. A minor one, but still, he'd never danced to Freddie's song before. Didn't matter. He could still win. "No problem, Fillmore! Doesn't matter the jam 'cause I'll still dance rings around you."

"You're on. Dance-off! Yeah! What's the winner—me—get?"

In the heat of the moment, Zach had forgotten his true mission. "If I win—and I will—you have to tell me the truth about something. My choice. If you win—fat chance, way fatter than Burly Brian—you can have my headline spots for two weeks."

First Freddie went all ga-ga, fame dancing around his head, stars in his eyes like a cartoon character. Then he squinted, a look of distrusting shiftiness. "What's this about, Caulfield?"

"You'll find out when I win. Unless you're chicken."

"Nobody calls Fireman Freddie a chicken! Especially a loser like you, Caulfield!"

"Only chicken I see here is wearin' a G-string. Cluck-cluck, Fillmore!"

That really got Freddie. He bumped Zach's chest again. "You're gonna so regret this, Caulfield. I'll be spotlighting from now on."

"Bring it."

Burly Brian poked his fuzzy, flabby head between the curtains. "Um, hey there, Zach."

"Brian." Zach kept his eyes on Freddie.

"Hey, Freddie, you coming or what?"

"Fire up my jam, Brian." Zach hated when Freddie used that unfunny pun. Over and over again. "We're having a dance-off!"

Burly Brian's jaw dropped. "A…dance-off. Wow! Okay, cool, you got it!" He vanished like a groundhog on his namesake day.

Soon, the overly familiar chords of Freddie's tiresome jam began. One Zach never truly understood. Weren't dancing songs supposed to be seductive?

A squeal came out of the speakers before Burly finally got it together. "Ladies and more ladiesssss! Tonight's a verrrrry special occasionnnnnn!" Not only did Brian dance like a clumsy wrestler, he even announced like one. "A dance-offffff!" Cheers and screams, true music to Zach's ears. "Between Fireman Freddieeeee! And the Banana Hammock Bandittttttt!"

Zach took several deep breaths. Fortified himself by flexing his muscles, holding the pose until his arms and shoulders shook. Freddie did the same thing. They stared at one another, both trembling, faces turning red. A game of chicken. Zach released first. This wasn't the challenge he needed to win. A cleansing breath. Then he kicked his leg high, barely missing Freddie's chin. Freddie reciprocated. One last chest-bump before show time.

Onstage, the opening chord rattled the speakers. Freddie pranced out through the curtains, swinging his hips like a drag queen. For once, Zach was forced to watch Freddie's joke of a routine from backstage.

"We didn't start the fireeeee...."

With his plastic axe slung over his shoulder, Freddie strolled across the stage. In his first cliché move he held his hand over his eyes and peered coyly out into the audience. Then he tossed the axe in the air, quickly shed his fireman's coat and caught the axe on its downfall. Unbelievably, the crowd went wild. They hadn't seen anything yet, not until Zach's turn.

Get in the zone, in the zone, in the zone. Feel the beat. Make it you, be the beat...

Zach jumped onstage, beginning with a spin. Landed with his butt facing the adoring audience. Tighten and shake! Two of his best assets. The kid gloves came off. Body to the left, body to the right, twist! With his profile facing the audience, he launched into a body roll. His shoulders rotated back, the music moving into his tight abs, down to his flat-board stomach, out through his body. Draw back, wait...hold it...hold it...face the audience. Hit it! *Groin thrust!*

"It was always burning since the world was turning..."

Many more cheers, lots more than Freddie got. To show his appreciation, Zach pulled off his t-shirt, twirled it, tossed it over his shoulder. *Take that, Freddie!*

Freddie looked pissed, fuming like a child. He turned, landed in a lame squat, hands on knees. Wiggled his butt. Over the music, Zach heard the plastic pants snapping like milk on cereal. Freddie glanced over one shoulder in a shy, teasing, embarrassing way, then over the other. Had the gall to put his fingertips to his lips like a bashful schoolgirl. Then he whipped off the plastic pants, worming his butt cheeks all over the stage.

The agony! My eyes!

Based on the audience's shockingly enthusiastic response, though, they were already three sheets to the wind. Drunk women would go nuts over anything. Hence Burly Brian's constant employment.

"We didn't start the fireeee…"

They want a show? I'll give 'em a show. Time to pull out the big guns.

Hip roll! Undulating pelvis bones always proved a favorite. Now to show the goods. Purposefully, Zach strutted across the stage—*his* damn stage—and stopped in front of Freddie. Freddie grabbed his shoulders, trying to move him aside. Like a statue, Zach stayed cemented. All's fair in the male entertainment dancing business. Another hip roll…and…*pants off*! The crowd went wild, women whistling, yelling, standing. In the moment, Zach tossed his pants into the crowd.

"No we didn't light it but we tried to fight it…"

Freddie scrambled, panicked. Almost like a noobie firefighter facing his first fire. He pulled out his hose, always his go-to prop when all else failed. The hose wrapped around his leg, then he turned into it, a dervish, until the hose enveloped his chest. He dropped the end between his legs, wagging it at the audience. So ho-hum, been there, done that. But apparently, it was a new audience. Because they cheered.

"We didn't start the fireeee…."

Last chorus of the song. Big finish! Zach dropped to the floor on his hands and toes, push-up position. With a hop, he spread his legs out, tenting onto his fingertips. Groin undulating, he graced the floor and back up again. *Riding the pony*! Flipped over on his back, never letting his butt touch the floor. Pelvis up, rolling into his back, his butt. Then *boom, boom*! Two explosive pelvic hits!

The song ended. Zach sprang to his feet amidst a massive rainstorm of green. He did his signature twirl, ended with a graceful bow, one that would make even his parents proud. As per custom, both he and Freddie walked the edge of the stage as women paid their appreciation. Zach glanced at Freddie's G-string (not that he was in the habit of doing that, mind you!), and noticed his was less packed full of bills.

Zach won! Not that there'd ever been any doubt, far from it.

Zach looked around for Zora. He saw her at the bar, both hands filled with drinks. Her eyes were wide and her mouth open. He'd shown her this time. Stripper? Hardly. Male entertainment dancer? Hellz *yeah*!

Burly Brian burst over the microphone, a thunderous vocal mess. "What say you, ladiesssssss? What a show!" Zach took another bow. "I'd have to give the first round to Fireman Freddie for his—"

"Oh, who asked you, Brian?" yelled Zach.

Brian cupped his hand over the microphone. "Um...sorry about that, Zach." He unleashed his hand along with his wrestler's rattle. "But the overall winner of the Bone-In Beef Club dance-off is the Banana Hammock Bandittttttt!"

Freddie, always a poor loser, cried at Brian, "What do *you* know, Brian? You're at *least* ten percent body fat!"

Bombastic, beautiful applause drowned out Freddie's whining. More bills filled Zach's G-string, more of the usual. But Zach still had his eye on the prize, forget about this bonus cherry on top. He approached Freddie.

"Time to pay the price, Fillmore," yelled Zach.

"That wasn't fair! You cheated! I had a bad night!"

"Sure you did. Like every night, right?"

"Up yours, Caulfield. I'm a better dancer and you know it!"

"Yeah, yeah, yeah. Tell it to the hand." Zach held his hand up in front of Freddie's face, a quarter inch away from making him lick his palm. "Time to spill."

"Fine. Whatever. Whaddaya wanna know?"

"Whatever you can tell me about Misty Meadows."

For once, Freddie lost his bluster. His mouth formed an "O." So did his eyes. He gulped. Then he did something completely unexpected.

He turned, leapt off the stage. Drinks spilled. The mob of adoring women parted. Shocked, Zach couldn't register what got into Freddie until he saw his glowing white ass-cheeks hightail it out the door.

Zach jumped down into the gathered crowd. "Sorry, excuse me…sorry…coming through!" When he reached the bar, he grabbed Zora's arm. "Come on, sis! The killer's getting away!"

Zora downed one drink, set the full drink on the counter. Then she shrugged, picked up the second one and chugged it.

Zach couldn't wait. He collided with a waiter, knocking over the drinks on his tray.

"Crap! Sorry, Ed!" But now manners didn't matter.

Clad only in his banana hammock, he burst through the front door. Cheers from the waiting line of women spread. Even though time was crucial, he'd never leave a fan wanting for more. Very unprofessional. Quickly, he spun, ending with a bow. Cameras raised, click-click-clicking his photo. Publicity like this couldn't be bought.

As he raced past the women, he tossed out, "The famous Banana Hammock Bandit! Appearing four nights a week at the Bone-In Beef Club!" At the end of the waiting line, he stopped, looked around for Freddie.

There! Crossing the street!

Freddie's bouncing, pasty buttocks stood out in the night like twin moons. Zach tossed off one more "Come and see me, ladies!" before setting out again in pursuit.

The parking lot gravel bit into his feet.

"Ouch! Crap! Dammit!" He tried hopping, tenderly setting down the balls of his feet. Finally, he resorted to tiptoeing quickly through the lot as if walking on coals.

In the street, a car's tires screeched. The car came to a halt, the fender barely missing Freddie.

Once Zach hit the smoother street pavement, he kicked into high speed, arms pumping with power. Dollar bills fluttered from his G-string, green butterflies. The car that had missed Freddie still sat at a stop, the driver behind the wheel shaking his head. At full speed, Zach turned sideways, legs out cannonball style, jumped across the hood. His bottom landed flatly mid-hood, stopping him. His cheeks burned.

It never happened to Hasselhoff that way, he always slid right over. He turned to the windshield behind him, yelled, "It's okay, sir! I'm a professional male entertainment dancer!" It felt awesome to say it, his clout holding the weight of a cop. He scooted off the hood and broke into a manic sprint.

Ahead, Freddie tripped on the curb, howled. His knee jerked up and Freddie wrapped his hands around it while he hopped. Zach hurdled over the curb, cutting the gap between them. A cool breeze kissed his burned cheeks and raised goose pimples. But mostly the chase had kick-started his adrenaline, spiking it into the stratosphere. Maybe he *would* make an awesome cop. An imaginary, thundering soundtrack accompanied his feet beating down on the sidewalk.

Freddie glanced over his shoulder, gave him a startled look. Then he tore off again, forgetting about his stubbed toe.

"Put some clothes on!" yelled an elderly woman.

"Official entertainment business, ma'am, nothing to worry about!"

They weaved between the strollers, the shoppers, a serpentine maze. Every time Freddie looked behind him, he slowed, allowing Zach to gain.

Someone screamed, a woman.

"No need to fear, ma'am! I'm on the side of right!"

Freddie practically dug his heels to a halt, then bounced a few more steps across the sidewalk, arms flagging in the air. He righted himself and dove into an all-night corner market.

Zach yanked the door open. Above him, a bell tinkled. At the sound his head practically retracted like a turtle into a shell. But his testicles absolutely withdrew deep within his banana hammock when he saw the shotgun pointed at him.

"Get outta my store, creep!" A teenage girl hoisted a gun nearly as big as her.

"Whoa, whoa, whoa! Easy, miss! I—"

"Don't call me 'miss,' pervert! I tol' you to get out!" She raised the gun higher.

"*What?* I'm not a pervert! I'm a male entertainment—"

"You're wearing nothing but dirty underwear!"

"No, no, no! This is my banana hammock, custom-made with dark spots to look like a banana. I'm just—"

Shreeeeeeeeee!

The whistle appeared out of nowhere as if she'd had it in her mouth all along. Zach winced, his hands over his ears.

"No, wait, you don't understand! I—"

"You've got three seconds to leave before I blow your banana hammock all over the canned goods!"

Bang!

For a minute, Zach thought he'd been shot. But when he opened his eyes, Heaven looked peculiarly like the corner market he'd just left his mortal coil in. Then he realized the cracking sound had come from the back of the store. Freddie leaving by the back exit.

"Sorry to have bothered you, miss! I'll give you free tickets to the Bone-In—"

"Get out, get out, *get out*!"

Blam!

This time she fired. Just over Zach's head. Behind him cans toppled, rolling over his feet. Smoke twisted up from the end of the barrel. The discharge his starter gun, Zach bolted.

"Get out, pervert! Get out, get out, get out!"

Zach careened down the narrow hallway, bumping into the bathroom door and rebounding through the exit door. It opened onto an alley, lit by a rectangle of moonlight at the end. Spotlighted within the alley exit were Freddie's ever-jiggling, luminescent butt cheeks. Guy really needed to visit a tanning booth.

He vanished around the corner. Zach rose up on tiptoes again, avoiding debris as he tottered toward the street.

Horns blared as he bounded out onto the sidewalk. To his right, Freddie was bent over, hands on knees, hyper-ventilating like Burly Brian after a set.

"Filmore, dammit! Stop!"

"Never!" Freddie straightened, lifted a foot and turned. But he'd slowed, winded by smoking. Still in the race, though. Zach threw out his arm. His fingertips grazed Freddie's back. Suddenly Freddie stopped. Zach bounced into him, tumbling them both to the sidewalk.

"Ooof!"

"Get offa me, Caulfield!"

"Not 'til you honor the bet, Filmore!"

Caught in a tight embrace, they rolled along the sidewalk, Freddie on top, then Zach. Zach held one of Freddie's arms down, raised his other hand, opened it in a slapping position.

"Not the face, not the face!" cried Freddie.

"I'll slap you so hard in the face it'll bruise unless you tell me what I want to know!"

"Fine! Jesus! Fine!"

Not trusting him, Zach collapsed on top of Freddie, pinning him to the sidewalk with his body. Plus he needed to rest, not that he'd ever admit it to Freddie. Around them, people had gathered, some filming with their phones.

Zach glanced up, plugged in his mega-watt smile. "The one and only Banana Hammock Bandit, ladies, appearing four nights a week at the Bone-In Beef Club!" He turned his attention back toward Freddie. "Now…what do you know about Misty Meadows? Why'd you run?"

"We…we…" Freddie struggled, gave up. He gulped, closed his eyes. "We're…Furries!"

The notion stunned Zach. His jaw dropped. His world spun. Not necessarily because Misty and Freddie were Furries.

But the gall they'd never invited him to join—not that he would've—was just too much to fathom.

The alcohol Zora'd downed had made her light-headed. Probably not the wisest move, no doubt about it. But she'd needed something—*anything*—to eradicate the nightmare she'd just suffered. Her brother performing a strip tease! *Gross!*

She stumbled through the seedy streets surrounding the strip club, chasing after her idiot brother, while he streaked after his playmate.

She saw Zach dash into a small market. Preparing for the worst, she entered with her hand on the pistol in her purse.

Yep. The worst.

She smelled cordite, saw the wounded cans on the floor. And the terrified—no, scratch that, wildly pissed off—store clerk. Funny, her brother had that effect on people often. She leaned over the counter, chin sunk in her hands, and shook her head at the mess before her. A shotgun lay on the counter.

"Um, hey," said Zora, "you see two strippers come in here?"

She hitched a thumb to the right. "Went out the back door."

"Yeah, doesn't *that* just figure?"

Zora entered an alley and followed the commotion to the end of it. A small group of people were gathered on the sidewalk, their heads bowed down like scientists making a reverent discovery. Leave it to Zach to find an audience.

"Excuse me, pardon me…" Zora squeezed through the lookie-loos and immediately wished she hadn't. On the ground, Zach and Freddie were embracing one another, Zach's chin resting on Freddie's shoulder. "Why, hello, lovers!"

Zach looked around as if just now noticing the onlookers. He jumped to his feet. "What? *No!*" His hands went up, shaking like a presidential candidate trying to quiet his enthusiastic followers. "Ladies, we're *not* lovers! Fireman Freddie and I are as straight as arrows and—"

"Damn straight!" Freddie hopped up, dusted off his buttocks and flung a grotesque wink toward a woman to prove it.

"Uh-huh. Right," said Zora. "Tell it to the people who're gonna post this all over the internet."

"Wait… Sis, you don't really think they're gonna think we're—"

"You tell me, Zach! You guys are wrestling around, practically naked, lying on top of one another! Doesn't take a brain surgeon—or a stripper, for that matter—to connect the dots." Great payback for what Zach had put her through today.

Zach and Freddie shared a look, rich with deep humiliation and burgeoning fear.

But fun-time needed to end. "Okay, folks, show's over. Go home, post your videos about the gay strippers who—"

"Zora!"

"Hey, uncool!" chimed in Freddie.

"You know what's uncool? I'll tell you what's damned *uncool*! You guys racing through the streets with your butts flapping about! That's what's *uncool*!"

"My butt doesn't flap, Zor!"

"*Whatever!* Now, both of you, just shut up! And let's go somewhere a little more private to sort this out!" She stalked off to the alley, then turned. "Coming, girls?"

Suddenly self-conscious, Zach placed one hand behind him, the other in front of his hammock. "Yeah." He and Freddie slithered into the alley behind her.

"Alright. What the hell's going on here? Freddie…it's Freddie, right?"

Freddie flexed a muscle, grinned. Zora wanted to smack the grin off his face. "Hey, darlin', you can call me 'The Fireman'!"

"Yeah, that's not gonna happen. And quit overcompensating for your sexual preferences."

"I'm not gay," mumbled Freddie.

"Tell it to YouTube. Why'd you run?"

"Cause Zach wanted to know about Misty. Misty Meadows. And I…didn't want our secret getting out."

"What secret?"

"That we're…Furries." He hung his head, a cowlick sticking straight up like a question mark.

"Furries? What the hell're Furries?" asked Zora.

"I'll take this one, Sis. Furries are fans of furry animals from, like, sci-fi and cartoons and crap. So they dress up like them. In big costumes."

"You've got to be kidding me. So, what? They crawl around and act like animals?"

"No, no," said Freddie, "we're, um, whaddaya call it? Promorph…no… Transformer…wait…poly-sexual. Crap, hang on, I'll get it…"

"Somehow I kinda doubt that. You mean anthropomorphic?"

Freddie tapped his nose. "Yeah, that's it! Told you I'd get it! We walk and act like people, but also sorta like animals. We like petting, hugging, scritching—"

"Yeah, I don't wanna even know. Okay, so it's super creepy and everything…but is that any reason to run butt naked through the streets?"

Suddenly, Freddie lost his cockiness. His shoulders caved in, his ego deflating. "It's…kinda bigger than that. Look, I became a Furry about three years or so ago. Just for, you know, kicks. Started going to conventions and—"

"There're conventions?"

"Oh, sure. Big business. Conventions, role-playing. My fursona's Foxy Freddie, by the way." Freddie paused and looked at Zora.

"If you're waiting for me to be impressed, not gonna happen. Get on with it already."

"Okay, okay. Zach, your sister's a real ball-breaker."

"Not yet, but that can be arranged. Now talk."

"Anyway…I knew Misty. Been goin' to her for massages for a while. Longer than Caulfield here." The two strippers glared at one another. "She'd been telling me how unhappy she was. I kinda think she was bored."

"So you had an affair with her?" asked Zora.

"No! Nothing like that. I'm a pro, after all, don't mix business with pleasure." Another slimy wink.

"What a gentleman."

"I know, right? Anyway…I thought Misty might get a kick out of joining me at some of the Furry gatherings. You know, just to give her an outlet and stuff."

"So…you started taking her to these…Gawd-awful things?"

"Hey, don't judge me!"

"Would you rather I busted my first set of balls?"

"No need to get hostile. Heh. Yeah, I took her. Now, most Furries are male, not too many chicks. So…the local Furries took a real liking to Misty. If you know what I mean." He dredged up a lusty chuckle and nudged Zach. "But…pretty soon, she wanted to go even further."

"Oh my God! How much more depraved can it get?" said Zora.

"Well…um, there's a faction of Furries. Not all of 'em, mind you! But some…like to have sex. In their costumes. There're actual sex meetings on a regular basis."

Zora tried not to let that picture form in her head but it formed anyway. "You have *got* to be *kidding* me! That's the sickest, foulest, most disgusting… You, Freddie? You're a part of this?"

"Me? No! But I know some of 'em. So…I, um, turned Misty onto the guys. I'd never go to the sex groups myself, though. Got a reputation to uphold and all."

"Oh, sure. Your stellar reputation."

"Thank you!"

"Sarcasm much, Freddie? Gah! Anything else? Does this get any worse?"

"Wellllllll, rumor has it…there're some powerful people in the Furries sex club. And they'll do anything to keep their identities secret."

Zora blinked. "Like who? And what're you saying? They'll kill people?"

Freddie shrugged. "I dunno. But scuttlebutt along the Furry pipeline—"

"There's a pipeline?"

"Uh-huh. And word is these guys will do anything! I don't wanna get involved."

"Who're these people, Freddie?"

"Dunno. And even if I did, I wouldn't tell you."

"You're such a wimp, Filmore!" Zach thrust out his chest, turned toward Freddie.

Freddie did the same until their chests bumped. "Yeah, right, Caulfield! I could take you with one arm tied behind—"

"Boys!" Zora clapped her hands, the sound echoing off the alley's brick walls. "Before you start making out again—"

"Didn't make out," groused Zach.

"*Whatever!* Let's get back to business. Freddie, where can I find these…ugh…sex meetings?"

Freddie looked at Zora, then Zach, tennis-balled back to Zora. "There's one tonight. It's what Misty told me last week. But that's all I know. Misty's going to it. Hell, just call her up and ask her."

Zach took Freddie by the shoulders. "You don't know, do you?"

"What? What're you talkin' 'bout, Caulfield?"

"Fillmore…Freddie…Misty's dead. Someone murdered her."

"Misty… No…can't be…"

"Sorry, Fillmore. But, yeah, it's true. We're trying to find her killer."

The strippers hugged, for once without the stupid posturing. And after seeing Freddie's reaction, Zora was certain he'd had nothing to do with the murders. But he was still sleazy and greasy.

"Alright, Freddie. Sorry for your loss. But will you help us find her killer? For Misty?"

"Yeah, crap, whatever. I'll do what I can. But I ain't goin' to that meeting."

"Fine. Can you get us in?"

"I think so. I know a guy—"

"Of course you do."

"And it'll cost ya."

"Of course it will." Zora glowered at Zach. He threw up his hands, idiotically feigning innocence.

"And," continued Freddie, "you're gonna have to dress up. As a Furry."

Zora looked to the Heavens and screamed, "Of *course* we are!"

Chapter Seven

For once, Zach didn't want the limelight. He used both hands to cover his bottom as he left the Bone-In Club and slunk past the party-line of giggling women toward his sister. And crap, Zora'd seen him already. He could see her eyes widen even through the windshield.

With a heavy sigh, Zach held the front seat forward while Freddie climbed into the back. Then he crawled in, ready to get a heaping spoonful of ridicule.

"Soooooo. What exactly *is* that you're wearing?"

"I don't wanna talk about it." Zach started the car, sinking into the upholstery and deeper into humiliation. "Just drop it."

"Hah! No way I'm dropping this! No way!"

He chucked the drive gear into park, turned in his seat. "Okay. Let's get it out in the open. Have your laugh."

From the backseat, Freddie snorted.

"Shut up, Freddie!" Zach turned in his seat and glared into the back. "You've caused enough problems for one night!"

"How?" Zora barely eked the word out between guffaws.

"Look, we went back in the Bone-In to get our clothes…but someone stole my tear-away pants So I had to borrow a, um, replacement."

"With the word 'Juicy' plastered on your ass? They look like Capris! They're women's sweatpants, Zach!" Zora laughed so hard her feet kicked the glove box.

"Enough! It's not like I coulda borrowed Burly Brian's pants, dammit! They'd be falling down all the time!" Freddie sniggered. Zach rearranged the mirror and glared at Freddie until he stifled it. "So…I had to borrow Shelly the bartender's spare sweats."

"Okay, Juicy! Let's go!"

"Oh, boy."

"Juicy Lucy, fresh and fruity!"

"Stop it!"

"Juicy! Juiceyyyyyy!"

"They were damn good tear-away pants, too," mumbled Zach. Hoping to change the subject, he added, "Still can't believe Misty never asked me to join the Furries."

Zora's laugh cut off in midstream. "You gotta be kidding me. I thought better of you, Zach!"

"Hey, never said I wanted to be a Furry. It…just woulda been nice to have been asked."

"Oh for… That's what's got your hammock in a bunch? Because the cool Furry kids didn't ask you to join their demented lil' club?"

"Well, I guess. Maybe." He didn't want to elaborate. But having been excluded from the cool kids during his rocky tenure in high school still hurt. "Just woulda been nice. All I'm sayin'."

"We wouldn't want you in the Furries, Caulfield!" said Freddie. "You're just—"

"Alright, both of you, enough. Freddie, take us to your guy."

During the drive, Freddie remained unusually quiet. Almost as if afraid. Zach knew Freddie was a chicken at heart but it bothered him. A cold chill ran down his back. His sweats seemed to tighten, crawling up into his crack.

Freddie leaned forward. "Okay, it's coming up. Turn in here."

Zach turned into a mass storage unit company. The sign read *Stop & Drop*. Not exactly what he'd expected for a covert meeting. And it sounded like a heart attack waiting to happen.

They pulled up to the gate and Freddie got out to type in his password on the security code pad. He kept looking over his shoulder to make sure Zack and Zora weren't peeking like *they* were the ones who couldn't be trusted. The gate lifted. Zach gunned the car forward a few feet to make Freddie run to catch them. Every time Freddie reached for the car door handle Zach shot the car forward again.

"Am I gonna have to drive, Zach?" asked Zora. "Play with your boy-toy on your own time."

"Not my boy-toy."

Freddie stood outside, hand on the door, to make sure Zach wasn't about to gun it again. Satisfied but still yet cautious, he slid in. "Real funny, Caulfield!"

"Funny like your face, Fillmore! Okay, sis. Let me handle this. I'll do all the talking." Zach thumped his chest.

"Yeah, I don't see that happening."

"Fine with me," said Freddie. "I'll stay in the car."

"Cluck, cluck, Filmore!"

"Up yours, Caulfield!"

A round figure, nearly as round as his height, stood by storage unit #312. Zach killed the headlights and parked the car. As soon as they got out, a flashlight blinded them.

"Um…Freddie sent us," called out Zach. "You Bart?"

"Ayup. That's what my friends call me. Ain't yet determined which category you fall into."

"Well…Freddie can vouch for us. Freddie Filmore?" Zach jerked a thumb toward the car. "He's in the car if you want to—"

"Wait! That little weasel's here? Never did like him!" Bart's voice rose into a growl.

"Hey, he's no friend of mine!" said Zach. "I don't like him either. But he said you have the, um…goods. And we brought money."

Zora shot him a look. Zach jutted out his lower lip, nodded satisfactorily with a patronizing hand up: *I got this, Sis.*

"All right then. I 'spose any money's good." He spat, sounding as sharp as gunfire in the deserted storage company lot. *Ker-splat!*

"Alright, Bart," said Zora, "let's see what you got."

Wheezing like an accordion, Bart mopped his shaved head and wrestled with the corrugated garage door. "Thing sticks once in a while. Here we go."

Gerrrrrr-runch!

Bart tugged a hanging light string. At the back of the unit, various animal pelts swayed on a mobile clothing rack.

"Here're my beauties," said Bart with a proud hand sway. "Treat 'em like their your babies. Course my wife won't let me keep 'em in the house. Says they're creepy."

"Imagine that," replied Zora.

"I know, right? But I always say a man's gotta have his hobbies."

Wire hangers scraped as Bart studied his trophy case. Zach looked over his shoulder, nearly expecting someone to jump in. From now on, he'd leave the cloak-and-dagger business to his sister.

"Young lady, I reckon you're a size small, that about right?" Bart ogled Zora, inventorying her weight.

"I can make it work," she said.

"Yeah, right," Zach said under his breath. Zora elbowed him. No way Zora wore small sizes, particularly after all the kids she'd had, but it'd probably be best to just let that slide.

"And you..." Zach's turn. "Medium?"

"No, large. But that's due to muscles, of course, not because of any body fat on—"

"Large, hmm? Only one I got left in a large is this." Bart lifted a costume off the rack, brought it to Zach.

Time for another round of humiliation. "A...bunny rabbit? Why do I have to be a—"

"Hey, only one I got right now in a large." Bart shrugged. "It's a popular costume. 'Benny Bunny.'"

"But...it's got long bunny ears!" Zach inspected the costume, holding it out at arm's length like a disgusting snake skin. "And...it's got a poofy tail on the back! And look at the eyelashes! They're long! Like a girl's!"

"Oh, suck it up, Zach! Be the bunny!"

Fine for his sister to say. She had a wicked-cool wolf costume, 'Willa Wolf.'

"Hey, Sis, just because you get a rockin' outfit—"

"Poor widdle bunny-wabbit!" She pouted her lips, raised her voice to a helium high. "Is poor widdle bunny-wabbit afwaid of the big bad wolf?"

"Okay. Knock it off—"

"Is being a bunny too icky for poor widdle Zachy?"

"Fine! I'll be the damn bunny!"

Bart just stared at the feuding siblings, head swinging back and forth. Still wheezing like an aspirator. Finally he said, "Hey, you know, I'm doin' you guys a favor by openin' up my warehouse this late and givin' you last minute costumes. If you don't want 'em, fine. But don't make fun of Benny Bunny, dammit!"

"Whoops. My bad. How much for the night, Bart?" Zora fished into her purse.

"Well, I'll give you a discount. Four hundred and fifty dollars each."

"$450.00! Come on!"

"Hey, it's usually five large! This is a steal! And 'course I'll need to get a credit card number and ID from you…in case you end up stealing my babies." He narrowed suspicious eyes.

"Yeah, I don't think that's likely," said Zora. "How much for two hours?"

"$450.00."

Zora sighed. "No negotiating? These friggin' things smell like they've been rented out by a football team! Dammit, Zach! You're gonna pay me back for this! Every last cent!"

"Hey, you know me, Sis. I'm good for it."

"Good for nothing, maybe. Fine Bart, done. But only if you supply some info as a bonus."

"Yeah? What's that?" Suddenly, his chest expanded like a blowfish, fists curled into ham hocks. Zach straightened, again preparing for battle.

"Freddie said you'd know where the big…um, sex party is tonight." She grimaced, wrinkled her face up as if she'd just bitten into a lemon. "The Furry one."

"Sure do. But it'll cost you." Three inches of height seemed to magically grow onto Bart's torso.

"Oh, for… Bart, look I already agreed to pay you nearly a thousand bucks. Which is stupid-ridiculous. I'll still pay you. But I'm not giving you a dime more. Just tell us where the party is."

Bart grinned. "No, ma'am, it's gonna cost you another $300 bucks."

Zora clicked her lips, shook her head. Pulled her phone out of her pocket. "Bart, Bart, Bart…I tried to do this the nice way. But long ago I learned to record 'iffy' conversations. Now, I'm not saying you're 'iffy' by any means…but a clandestine meeting at a storage until filled with God-awful smelling Furry costumes might be seen as 'iffy.' Particularly since you're offering advice as to where a sex party is. For money. Could be seen as extortion. Maybe even sexual trafficking. Who knows where the illegal part starts and ends. But I'm pretty sure your wife might be interested in your, ah…hobbies."

"You wouldn't—"

"I would. Because my patience is running thin and my blood pressure's running high! *So tell* me where this damn party is!"

"Okay, okay. Let's put our phones and threats away. We're all friends here." Bart waved his hands, deflating back into a pleasantly round and friendly costume peddler.

"Okay, BFF," said Zora, "like, what do you say you tell me where this fabulous party's happening? Speak, Bart, speak!"

"The Sheraton. Downtown. Next to the Crown Center mall. Suite #502. But you'll need the code word to get in."

"I'm all ears." Zora wiggled the wolf costume's ears.

"Um…it's 'Bi-Curious George.'"

Zora groaned. "Is *nothing* sacred anymore?"

Zora could practically smell the difference in the car after they dropped Freddie at the strip joint. But the stench of the costumes still overpowered any seedy aroma Freddie might've left behind. She glared at Zack. The things she did for him.

"What?" he asked.

"Why do I do this? Tell me, Zach, why do I go through such grotesque extremes to get your sorry butt off the hook?"

"Well…first of all, my butt's anything but sorry…" He tried smacking it, couldn't quite reach it in the compact car. "Second of all, you do it 'cause you love me, Sis."

True, even though she hated to admit it.

They pulled in front of Zach's apartment and got out, costumes in hand. "These costumes smell like crotch, Zach. Who knows what's gone on inside them, around them—"

"Welcome to the world of Furries. I guess." They entered the apartment. "It might not be all bad, Sis. I mean—"

"I don't want to know what you mean! Oh, hey, Carlos."

Carlos nodded, mumbled something behind his mouth gag. "Mmph-uh."

"If you have any intention of getting it on with a Furry, Zach, I'm out right now!"

"Come on, Sis...you know me better than that."

"I know you *too* well. Just go get dressed before I change my mind."

The cowl weighed heavily on Zora's head, hot and stale as morning breath. Through the eye holes she looked at her mirrored reflection. She had to admit she looked somewhat feral and ferocious, but a long way from sexy. She considered bringing it home. Maybe it'd scare some good behavior into the kids.

Zach, on the other hand, looked ridiculous. The costume's round, glassy eyes appeared ready to tear up any moment. One ear bent down, folded over the top of the head. A white belly centered the light gray costume.

"Well, guess I don't have to worry about you hooking up after all. Not in that getup. What's up, Doc?" Zora grinned.

"You're not gonna start again..."

"Oh, I haven't even started! It looks like a little girl's Halloween costume. All fluffy and puffy and cutesy and—"

"It's a guy's costume! Benny's a guy's name!"

"Yeah, so said Bart. You gonna trust him?"

Zach ran big, fluffy paws up his chest. "You don't think—"

"I do! Definitely a woman's costume!"

"Dammit! I can't go to the party like this! I'm—"

"You're going, all right. Think I'm about to go into that by myself?"

"Gah! Let's just get it over with then."

In the corner, Carlos watched them with calm curiosity. Hard to tell, though, *what* Carlos was looking at.

"Bye, Carlos," said Zora. "Hope to be back soon with some news."

"Bahhhhh," he said.

Zora realized they'd made a huge mistake. They really, *really* should've changed in the hotel's bathrooms.

Unable to fit through the hotel's revolving front doors, they had to wait until a doorman ushered them through a wider side door, carefully tucking their ears down to clear the sill. The doorman tried not to smirk but apparently had reached his breaking point. Zora mumbled something about going to a costume party. She fumbled at her purse, attempting to open it to give the man a tip, but her paws wouldn't comply.

On the way to the elevator, more lookie-loos stopped to take a gander, some with their phones hoisted high to preserve the moment. Frankly, Zora was happy for the anonymity her cowl supplied. Phillip wouldn't take too kindly to her being a dubious internet star.

She took advantage of the empty elevator and took off her cowl. Zach did the same thing, his hair standing up in a cowlick.

"How in the hell are people supposed to have sex in these costumes?" she asked.

Zach jabbed a paw toward his crotch, apparently having further investigated the "ins and outs" of his bunny suit. "You haven't seen the Velcro crotch patches? Tears away like that." Ludicrously, he attempted to snap his fingers.

"Um, can I just say *gag*?" As an afterthought, she gave Zach a dope-slap, but the padded paw didn't leave much impact. Or satisfaction.

"Maybe you should wear that all the time, Sis."

"I'll make up for it once we're human again."

"Still don't know why I have to be a stupid bunny rabbit…"

The elevator dinged. The doors whooshed back, exposing a long hallway. Music, laughter and the sounds of debauchery floated down the hall. Suite #502 pretty much occupied the entire eastern wing, only one other unmarked door lining the walls. They shuffled down the hallway, Zora's nerves ratcheting up high. She had no idea what to expect, what to find—perhaps, nothing—but she didn't truly believe that, not in her gut. Secrets were key to the unveiling of the Meadowses' murders and if they uncovered them at a Furry sex gathering, so be it. Just as long as nothing else became uncovered.

The costume provided a problem, though, one she hadn't realized until it was too late. No pockets for her gun. And she was going to have a hell of time getting it out of her purse with the clumsy wolf paws if she needed it.

In front of suite #502 stood a bear. Literally, a bear. Clearly over six-and-a-half feet tall. Furry arms folded over his chest. The bear's mask stared at them with solemnity. Or hunger. Zora couldn't decide which.

"What's up, Yogi? We're here for the party." As Zora reached for the door, a giant paw snagged her wrist. Of course *his* costume had dexterous fingers.

"Password?"

Zora hated to say it but she did. Maybe the library police wouldn't smite her down for the sacrilege. "Bi-curious George," she mumbled.

Big Bear nodded. "Okay."

"Don't get your head stuck in the honey-pot." Zora brushed by the bear and pushed open the door, ready to shield her eyes if necessary. Either the sex parties hadn't begun yet or the couples were in back rooms. *Thank you, God.*

A flurry of fur filled the room with not a single *human* in attendance. Even the waiters wore Furry costumes. Glasses clinked. A woman's shrill laughter clanged like a fire alarm. There were lots of lions, tigers and bears (*oh my!*) intermingled with varmints of a smaller variety, typically the type the lions and tigers and bears should be eating. A parade of skanky cats, clearly female, purred around in suits composed of rubber and fur. Some Furries were cartoonish with bugged out eyes and "whoopsy" mouths and others were positively grim with fierce fangs and cold predator eyes.

A chipmunk wearing a pint-sized top hat skittered up. He didn't say a word, just nuzzled against Zora's arm, nose riding the length of it.

"What the *hell*? Get offa me!" Zora took a step back and the chipmunk followed.

"Sis, he's—whaddaya call it?—scratching you."

"If he starts grooming me with his tongue, he's gonna get a tail end of buck-shot."

Still in character, the chipmunk straightened, paws bent down at the wrist. "Fine. Didn't wanna play with a wolf anyway," groused a man's voice. He scampered off at a trot, nudging up against one of the cat women.

"So far you're doing a bang-up job at being undercover, Sis. Remember what these people are here for," said Zach.

"I know. But we've got a different agenda. Come on, let's mingle." Before she could take a step, something pushed her into Zach.

A yellow dog held paws up to her face. A feminine voice apologized. "Sorry about that. I'm trying to get used to this tail." Somehow it wagged on its own, all three feet of it.

"Yeah, I can see that." Zora tried to capture the dog through her eye-holes, not the easiest task. "Come here often?"

"Oh, sorry. I don't swing that—"

"What? No…no, no, no, you don't understand. I—"

"Come here often?" Zach struck a pose in his bunny costume. With his chest out and shoulders back, his poof of a tail somewhat diminished the effect.

The dog relaxed. "My second party. Your first?"

Zach nodded, the bunny head slipping up to his chin.

"You're gonna love it!" Zora thought she heard her panting like a dog beneath her head gear. "Everybody's pretty easy-going and they make you feel right at home and—"

"Do you know Misty Meadows?" asked Zora.

Her cartoonish head swiveled back and forth between Zach and Zora. Finally, "Yes. We met at my first party. She sorta took me on… I was afraid and she helped introduce me around. Where'd I set my drink?" She twisted, again bumping her tail into Zora. Then she turned the other way, knocking a half-full glass over on an end table. "Oh, sorry!" She mopped the spillage up with a paw.

"Gotta watch that tail. Did Misty take any interest in anyone? Anyone special?"

A paw patted her mouth. "Yeah…him." She gestured behind Zora. A leopard, starkly white with black highlights, strolled out of a closed door, its cold blue eyes furrowed with menace. He strutted like he really was the king of the jungle, shoulders back, arms out as if he had muscle to spare. And like the lowly subjects in the pecking order of jungle survival, the other Furries gave him wide berth, scattering before him. A cat sidled up to him, claws roaming his chest, until he shoved her away.

Zora leaned in closer to the yellow dog. "Who is he?"

"Dunno. That's the deal here. We all remain in costume, no foul, no harm."

But harm had come to Misty and Martin Meadows. And what went on behind closed Furry doors had led up to it. Zora just knew it. "No clue at all?"

"No. Just that, I dunno, I think he's the organizer of these little get-togethers. Everyone seems to kiss his tail end." She yipped. Annoying habit. "Why're you asking about Misty, anyway? She's not here tonight. Unless she changed costumes. But I'm sure she would've talked to me."

Zora thought about lying to her, the easiest way to go. But she'd been Misty's friend—such as it was—and she deserved to know the truth. "Okay, what I'm about to tell you, you have to keep it quiet, okay?" Doggy nodded. "Don't freak out, remain calm and—"

"Oh my God..."

"Take it easy, okay? I really need you to remain cool and quiet—"

"Oh my God, no, no, nooooo!"

Well, crap.

Ms. Yellow Dog ran in place, turning in a circle. Her tail swept a lamp off the table.

Thump.

"Noooooo! Not Misty! No, please, no, not Misty-ee-ee-ee!"

More glasses swept off a table, cracking against one another like tossed dice.

Clack, click, clack.

"Hey, hey, be a good, quiet, little doggy now." Zora felt helpless, angry with herself over her mistake, but most of all very stupid for using childlike "doggy talk" on the woman. She tried to put an arm around the woman's shoulders, but her costume constricted her reach. "Zach! Help me! Do something!"

Zach cradled Ms. Doggie in his arms and led her to the sofa. He sat next to her, talking quietly, and definitely helping for once on this undercover mission. Just in time, too. When Zora turned back around, the leopard stood before her, locking her within the dead gaze of his costume eyes. Zora knew the eyes were glass, but they still chilled her. Intensity rippled through them like water.

"Um, hi."

"What in the world is going on here?"

Though muffled, Zora thought she recognized the voice. *Maybe.* She needed to be sure. "Ah…my friend just got some bad news. Through a text. Sick relative, I think."

"Huh. Funny…thought I heard her mention someone by the name of Misty."

"Oh. That's short for Melissa. Her cousin."

"But you just said you *think*. As if you don't know for sure."

"Kinda took us all by shock, I guess."

"You guess? You're not very sure of your convictions, are you, miss?"

"I'm sure of one thing." She didn't want to go there but couldn't think of any other diversion. Clumsily, she zipped a paw up his chest. "I like leopards."

"That a fact? I like foxes. You foxy?"

Gag. "I like to think so."

"Well, huh. Tell you what…it's hotter than Hades beneath this mask. What say we go somewhere a little more private, see what happens?"

Gotcha! The second time she'd heard the "hotter than Hades" expression today.

"I don't think so, Pastor Sparks."

"What? Dunno what you're talkin' 'bout, but I can absolutely swear I'm not this Pastor fella you think I am."

"Short term memory loss, maybe? Hope your memory stretches back to why you killed Misty and Martin Meadows."

One quick laugh—more like an animalistic snort—as he tipped his mask to the ceiling. He stared at Zora for a moment, stuttered a few words. Then, faster than his namesake leopard, he bolted out the door.

"Dammit! Zach," she called, "you're up! Hop, bunny, hop!"

Zach hadn't even managed to get the yellow dog's phone number before Zora started barking out orders. He looked up just in time to see the leopard vanish out the door. He sprung up off the sofa, turned around, said, "Sorry! Come find me at the Bone-In Beef Club four nights a week!"

He bumped into a zoo's worth of Furries before reaching his sister. She'd managed to get one of her paws off, now poking around in her purse.

"Hurry, Zach! It's our killer…Pastor Don Sparks."

"*What?* No way."

"Just go! I'll be right behind you."

Outside the room, Zach bumped into the door-bear.

"What's going on here?" growled the bear.

"Can't talk! Ah…hunting!" Zach maneuvered around him. Down the hall, Sparks tromped across the floor, headed for the stairwell.

Zach whisked after him, his legs chafing beneath the furry costume legs. His male entertainment legs. *Dammit.* At the stairwell door, Sparks paused, looked behind him. Then he cracked open the door and slipped through, his tail barely clearing as it closed with a *clomp*!

Panicked voices rose from the party, Zora's loudest of all.

"Get him, Zach!"

"Whaddaya think I'm trying to do?"

He reached the stairwell and kicked the door open cop style. He jumped through and landed in a squat. He looked down into the stairwell and saw the bright white of Sparks's costume glowing two floors below. *No problemo!* He'd hop over the railing just like Hasselhoff would do and make up some time.

"Aghhh!"

Uh-oh. Problemo.

His right foot twisted and turned into a bag of cement. But he couldn't stop. He pulled up his big bunny suit and ran, hopped, skipped, and jumped down the stairs. Light opened onto the bottom landing. Door hinges groaned. If memory served correctly, the door led into the hotel lobby.

Pain hadn't set in on the twisted foot yet; it just felt like a clumsy weight. He dragged it down the remaining steps, hoping he wouldn't damage it more. A woman screamed when he opened the bottom door. Sudden light from the lobby dazzled him, sending specks swirling in a vortex. When his vision cleared, he saw Sparks running toward the stores. The Crown Center stores, a labyrinth of twisting corridors, stairwells and hallways that Zach always had a hard time navigating. The hotel guest Sparks had knocked down in the process yelled after him.

Zach curled and danced his way around the lobby guests. "Excuse me! Sorry! No need to panic, ma'am, I'm on official murder business!"

Someone screamed again. Maybe he should've phrased his "business" better.

Zach turned the corner into the maze of stores. All closed. Only a bare minimum of lighting illuminated the hallway. Tiny random dots of red lights looked down upon him like werewolf eyes. Shivers slalomed down his back.

A couple, hand in hand, met him when he turned the corner.

"Dude, you looking for a leopard?"

"Yeah."

"He went that way." The kid jacked a thumb over his shoulder.

"Thanks for being a good citizen, um…citizen!"

"Whatever, dude."

Zach ran down the hallway, now favoring his wounded paw and pretty much skipping. Voices bubbled up. The blessed light grew stronger. He raced up a short, wide flight of stairs to the sounds and sights of civilization. A large group of people sat on a children's café terrace next to the escalators.

A child cried out, "Mommy! The Easter Bunny!"

Zach turned in a half-circle and called out, "I'm not the Easter Bunny! Drink milk, stay in school, exercise!"

"Are too the Easter Bunny! You're hopping!"

Zach swept his gaze aground, then looked up. Sparks stood on the last steps of the escalator, trying to catch his breath. Zach was tempted to give his foot a rest and just ride the escalator, but couldn't risk it. At least he had the railing to hoist himself up. He glanced down as he neared the top. Zora burst into the lobby, waving her gun around. Which prompted more screams.

"Don't you kill the Easter Bunny!" yelled a kid.

"Donny! Stop!"

A small mob of children broke away from the café. *Damn!* Running for Zora. Zach hesitated, but he had a killer to catch. Zora could hold her own. She'd have to.

Sparks slowed to a near crawl. He turned into another darkly lit corridor and slipped away into shadow. Zach stopped, focused. Listened. Entered the zone. No sound, not a peep.

Zach approached the corridor and glanced into a pen shop's glass window. He nearly shrieked. A large hideous bunny with bedroom eyes smiled at him. His reflection had turned into the stuff of emasculating nightmares.

From the darkness, a growl burbled low and grew into a snarl.

"*Why* can't you *leave me be*? I'm doing God's work, damn you!" Sparks jumped out of a store's alcove and wrapped an arm around Zach's neck. Zach stumbled back. His foot caught and they both fell, Sparks on top of him.

"*Oof!*"

Zach spread his legs out and closed them around Sparks's back. He had the upper body strength advantage and he could use it. He wrenched Sparks's arm from around his throat, held him up by the shoulders and punched where he judged his chin to be. Like hitting a plush sofa, Sparks remained unaffected.

A tide of children's laughter intermixed with angry shouts grew like a buzzing swarm of bees.

"Freeze, Sparks!" Zora stood, legs spread, mask off and gun locked in both hands. One kid latched onto her leg. Others pulled at her costume.

"Don't you hurt the Easter Bunny, lady!"

"He's not the one I'm gonna hurt! Now let go!"

Sparks stopped struggling, rolled over, moaned. "It's all over, all of it, my dynasty, my…"

Zach jumped up and cringed when he landed on his bad foot. "See, kids," he said. "I'm okay. Oh, and don't do drugs."

The kids didn't care, though, too wrapped up in contagious mob behavior.

Zora yelled, "Parents! *Please* come get your kids!"

It took some time for Zora to straighten everything out with hotel security and the recently arrived street cops. Who would've thought "Willa Wolf" lacked credibility? When he got there, Soundtrack Saul vouched for her. After creeping everyone out with one of his song and dance routines, of course. But security still hovered over Zora as she interrogated Sparks, apparently afraid of the big bad wolf.

"Okay, Pastor…" Tired, hot, sweaty and sick of the damn wolf costume, she sat down next to him. "…why'd you do it? Kill Misty and Martin Meadows?"

"What? I didn't kill Misty! I didn't even *know* she was dead 'til I heard it on the news! Why, I loved that girl!" He sat up, his eyes glinting around the edges.

"Could've fooled me. Innocent people don't run."

"I'm innocent in the eyes of the Lord, yes, indeed!" Fully back on his turf, he raised his voice along with his hands.

"Save it for the jury, Sparks. Why'd you kill them?"

"And I'm telling you I had nothin' to do with poor Misty's demise. As I said…I loved that girl. You check with my assistant, Katherine. She can tell you I was there at the church all morning when someone took poor Misty's life."

"Assistants are willing to lie. 'Spose it depends on how much you're paying her."

"That's just…cockadoodie! Excuse my language. But if you won't take her word for it, I can give you the names of several parishioners who I met with."

"I'm sure the police will check that out." Something sank in Zora's stomach like an anchor. The long night hadn't ended yet, after all. "What about Martin Meadows?"

Good-naturedly, the pastor grinned. Then licked his lips as if relishing the taste. "Well now, him I did do away with. Had to knock out his old nosy sister, also, but to make an omelet and all that."

"Why'd you kill him?"

"He found out Misty was coming to our call-to-gratification meetings."

"Call-to-gratification meetings? That's how you're sugar-coating it?"

"You wanna hear my story or not, young lady?"

"Undoubtedly." Zora drew up her knees, comfy for story-time.

"Anyway…I dunno how her husband found out about the meetings. Misty claims she didn't tell him. And I believed her. Girl didn't know how to lie. But Martin started raising a holy ruckus, threatening to expose our meetings if she didn't quit coming. Misty was ready to quit, but I wasn't ready for her to do so. So—"

"Wasn't your decision."

"Excuse me?"

"Her life. Her decision on what to do with it."

"Feminist claptrap. Anyhoo…I decided to take matters into my own hand. So Misty could keep comin' to the meetings. Keeping my second flock together."

"Ugh. Can't believe some of the crap that comes out of your mouth. So…were you having an affair with Misty?"

"What? Course not, young lady! What kinda heathen do you take me for? Course I mighta lusted in my heart a little bit for her…" The moisture in his eyes dried up, replaced with a far-off look of desire. "…but we're all sinners in God's eyes."

"You more than anyone, Pastor."

"How dare you? I'm a dang good pastor!"

"So you followed us earlier today? On Metcalf?"

"Wasn't exactly me, of course." He grinned, happier than a pig in slop. Pretty much looked like one, too. "Had one of my faithful keepin' an eye on y'all."

"How'd that work out for you?"

"Listen here, young missy, I—"

"Don't call me 'young missy'!"

"You prefer I call you 'ol' missy'?"

Zora nearly blew a gasket, considered popping the pastor one. But with the mob of children still trying to push through police lines, she thought better of it. "Don't call me anything at all. You haven't earned the right."

"So sayeth you." She almost responded with "I do sayeth," but realized it'd sound a little too Elmer Fuddian. "My faithful will still believe in me. All I was tryin' to do was keep my church together. A little scandal like this woulda rocked a lot of people's worlds! And you have the gall to sit there and judge me—"

"Damn guilty!" She slammed her fist down, a mock gavel. "That's how I judge you. Not only of murder and numerous other crimes, but also of being the biggest hypocrite of them all." She tried to jump to her feet to make a dramatic exit. But the damned costume impeded her progress. Instead she rolled over on her belly, scrabbled to hands and knees and finally managed to make it to her feet. Worse than an unsteady baby learning to stand. So much for drama. "Later, Pastor. Enjoy your born-again prison status."

Chapter Eight

After a quick change out of the sweat-soaked Furry costumes and assurances to Carlos they'd only be a bit longer, they crawled back into the Trans Am. Even though Zach suspected his sister didn't have a destination in mind. He patted his trusty steed, Becky, mentally implored her to get them through the night.

"Alright, we still have some work to do. Damn night's never gonna end," groused Zora.

"Negativity causes premature wrinkling," said Zach. "Hey, we're 50% in the clear!" To double-check his math, he counted off the digits on one hand. Twice. "Yep, halfway home!"

"That's not *good* enough, Zach."

"Don't blame me. Again…none of this is my fault. Besides, I have bigger issues to worry about now. My foot's starting to swell up to the size of a football. Gah. How am I supposed to entertain the ladies while dragging around a foot's worth of Burly Brian's weight onstage?"

"That's what you're worried about? *Really?* Hello! Number one suspect in Misty Meadows's murder!"

"But…I thought they cleared me, sis! You had the camera evidence of when I entered and left the motel room!"

"That was before you decided to piss off Soundtrack Saul. Now he's got a real mad-on for you. Barely got out of that Crown Center scrape. Probably wouldn't have had Saul not been so tickled to make an arrest in Martin Meadows case. Guy likes to close 'em with as little work and as much singing and dancing as possible."

"Can't sing or dance."

"And you can't seem to shut up. How many times did I tell you not to mention his…stuff?"

"Sorry, sis. Really. But when I see something like that, I just have to speak up. It's, like, it hurts my guts. Or something."

"Poetic."

"Thanks. So…is there any way Pastor Sparks could've murdered Misty?"

Zora stared out the car windshield, her eyes glassy. "Doubt it. I mean, he readily confessed to Martin Meadows's murder. Which was kinda weird, really. Been my experience getting a confession outta these guys is like extracting teeth. When you think about it, he had a lot to lose, yet he confessed nonetheless. Why would he cover up a second murder he perpetrated? I'll slow down if I'm using too many big words, Zach."

"Yeah, like that's possible."

"Oh, I forgot you're a Rhodes Scholar."

Zach blinked. "What? You mean like…one of those highway engineers? Sis, you know I'm a male entertainment—"

"Stripper. Yeah, yeah, yeah. Heard it all be—"

"Male entertainment dancer."

"You know, for once I'm just gonna ignore you. Don't know why I haven't learned that lesson before. Anyway…as I was saying, Sparks confessed to Martin's murder. If he truly murdered Misty—which I don't think he did—then one more murder tossed on his rap sheet wouldn't make that big a difference. Not these days. No, he didn't do it."

"What about Carlos? Or Della?"

"Zach, they're so brain-fried, they probably can't even tie their shoes, let alone murder someone."

"Then…what do we do now?"

She said nothing. She'd entered her zone, the mental zone.

Didn't take her long to surface. Never did. He'd never tell her—unless it was a deathbed confession and he hoped tonight wouldn't end like that—but he was damned proud of her, and *really* glad to have her watching his back. Still, siblings have to keep up the façade of disliking one another.

"Crap. Sparks said someone told Martin Meadows about Misty's involvement with the Furries sex club."

"Yeah?"

"Who do you think might've done that?"

"Um…"

"Never mind. Let me look up something." She pulled out her phone, her fingers tapping away. "Got her."

"Got who?"

"Who had Martin's ear?"

"Nobody! He had both his ears when he—"

Whack!

"Ouch! What was *that* for?"

"Because you keep interrupting me by saying stupid things."

"You asked—"

"Melora, idiot! Martin's sister, Melora Meadows! She watched him like a hawk and I'm sure he confided everything to her. And she to him. I found her on Linked In. Guess what she does for a living? No, don't even bother. She's a nurse. At Shawnee Mission Hospital."

"Okay. Swell, whatever. You gonna befriend her?"

"I'm gonna unfriend you permanently if you don't quit interrupting. You remember how Misty died?"

"Um…oh, *snap*! Slaphappy Saul said it looked like she'd been injected with something before she was suffocated. Her nursing background!"

"Give the boy a golden star!"

"What about her alibi?"

"That was stupid, sloppy on my part. I left that to the cops. Figuring if there was a discrepancy, Saul'd let me know. Hang on, let me call him…" Saul picked up right away. "Saul, what was Melora Meadows's alibi?... Uh-huh, what I thought… Do yourself a favor and check the hospital's security camera footage at all of the exits and entrances to the hospital this morning… Nothing. Just a hunch… But I'll bet you'll see Melora sneaking out during her shift… Hospitals are big places. Her fellow employees probably don't know where Melora is half the time.

God knows patients never know where nurses vanish to... Right. Hit me back." She hung up, gloating. "We have no real proof. But let's go lie our butts off."

Twenty minutes later, they pulled into Martin Meadows's driveway. The house was well lit, almost urgently so.

"What now, sis?"

"We're gonna go ring the doorbell, what the hell you think?"

Absolutely thrilled, Zora hustled to the door, Zach dragging his foot behind her. By the time he caught up to her, she was pounding the door with her fist.

The curtain in the small window pulled back. A bespectacled eye peeked out. "Go away," Melora shrieked. "I'm in mourning. Leave me to grieve!"

"Sorry to bother you again, Miss Meadows, but this is important." Zora continued rapping her knuckles. "I'm not going away. As soon as we talk to you, we'll leave!"

The door whipped open. "Dang your eyes! I told you I'm mourning! Why don't—"

"Does your mourning involve a vacation?"

Melora's eyes widened. "Excuse me?"

Zora pointed over her shoulder. "Suitcase. Going somewhere?"

"That's none of your business, young lady! I'm going to call the police now. You're trespassing."

"Go right ahead, Miss Meadows. I'm sure they'd love to know why you killed Misty."

Like a baby trying to form words, her lower lip dropped, bouncing in silence. "That's quite enough! How dare you? I'm calling them right this moment!" She swiveled on her heels and walked down the hall.

Zora made a *let's go* gesture. She led the way, Zach sliding down the hallway after her like Igor.

From behind a half-closed door, Melora's voice rose.

"That's right... Two intruders in my house... Please hurry! I think they might be dangerous..."

Zach saw it on his sister's face, the first look of doubt she'd registered all day. But confidence pushed that dark cloud away. Cautiously, she placed her fingers on the door and opened it.

"Come right in. Took you long enough," said Melora. But now she wasn't alone. She held a friend: a big, honking, scary, metallic friend pointed in their direction. The church lady had transformed into Dirty Harriet.

Zora groaned, tossed her hands up. "Not again."

Zach followed her lead, putting his hands up. He needed to wait, plan the right moment to bust a move. Problem was his foot didn't feel up to cooperating.

WWHD? What would Hasselhoff do?

"Step into the room now. Carefully, slowly."

Like Zach could do it any other way.

"Why'd you kill Misty, Melora?"

"Because she was an awful harlot! My word! My brother was too good for her! But he didn't want to go through the shame of a divorce. And in his own way, I suppose he did love her. Hard as that is to believe. But when I found out she was a masseuse—a masseuse, mind you!—I just had to tell Martin—"

"Excuse me, Miss Meadows, but Misty was a massage therapist, not a—"

"Shut up!" Zora and Melora yelled it simultaneously, a mean chorus. Outnumbered, outgunned, Zach complied.

"Martin didn't believe me at first. That's when he consulted you, Miss LeFevre. As if my word wasn't good enough for him! Then the next day, I found out Misty was involved with those...ghastly fuzzy heathens! My word!" Her free hand fluttered to her heart. "Then I just had to make Martin listen to me!"

"How'd you find out about the Furries?" asked Zora.

"Why, straight from the horse's mouth! Not that it's any of your business. But I'd heard gossip around the church about such horrendous goings on. Sex clubs and such. And Misty's name had been mentioned. So I asked her myself. You know what she said in defense of herself? Do you?" She wagged the gun. Zach flinched.

"You have the gun," said Zora. "I assume you're gonna tell us anyway."

"She raised her voice to me! To *me*! Said how unhappy she was, that she didn't even know who she was, that she felt everyone in her life had tried to form her into something she wasn't, something they wanted her to be. All sorts of Satanic new age baloney!"

"She was right, Miss Meadows," said Zora. "Her parents forced her into Benito's Bandits. She didn't have a say. Then Martin pressured her into—from what I can gather, a fairly passionless marriage."

"Martin did *not* pressure her!" Her arm locked rigid, the barrel looming larger. "She was more than willing to ride the coattails of Martin's success, lying about the house, doing nothing all—"

"Martin wouldn't let her work!" Clearly pissed off on Misty's behalf, Zora lowered her hands. But Melora jacked them up again by nudging the gun.

"The way a marriage is supposed to be, young lady! None of this Godless claptrap you feminists spout on about!"

"You know, I'm *really* getting tired of being called a feminist today! And having guns pointed at me! Why don't you just lower—"

"I'll do no such thing. If I have to shoot you, I will. Everything I've done has been out of love for Martin."

"Killing Misty was an act of love?"

"Yes. I knew of the motel where she carried on her wanton ways. This morning, I set out, hoping to catch her in some wanton act of adultery. I sat outside, waiting. Thinking, deliberating my next course of action. Then like a Heavenly beacon, a God-sent beam of sunlight strayed into the car, alighting on my medical bag in the passenger seat. Honestly—and just between you, me and God—I wasn't supposed to have lifted the meds from the infirmary. But Martin had been having trouble sleeping and no one would miss a few sedatives and tranquilizers. But the message was clear. I gathered a hypodermic of the strongest sedative and trudged around to the alleyway. Very unladylike, mind you, but it took nothing at all to jimmy open her room's window and climb through. When Misty arrived and saw me, she looked hateful, just like the harridan I knew her for. Asked me what I wanted. I told her I just wanted to talk. But I injected her in the neck. She stumbled to the bed, fell into it. Soon fell asleep like a newborn babe. I had to finish the job. Suffocated her with a pillow. So ironic. I gently massaged the pillow over her face until Satan took her. She went peacefully."

"She shouldn't have gone at all, Melora!" Zach knew his sister was pissed now, skipping niceties such as surnames. "Just as in life, people decided how she'd live…and you, how she'd die!"

"Be that as it may, she deserved it."

"Oh, now you've really gone and ticked me off." Zora tossed on her invisible shield of invulnerability and took several steps forward.

"Don't, sis!"

"I'd listen to your brother if I were you."

Zora stopped. "Don't you even want to know who killed your brother?"

For a second, Melora lowered the gun. Zach thought about making his move. But he couldn't close the gap soon enough, not with his damaged foot. Not against a bullet.

"You know who did it?"

"Yes. I'll tell you if you put the gun down."

Melora took a few hesitant steps forward, yet the gun remained up and certain. "Tell me. Now!" She shuffled forward a couple more steps. Getting closer.

In anticipation, Zach started shuffling his feet. Well, one of them. He balled his upraised hands into fists. Melora came close enough for him to dart and dive. But his gentlemanly upbringing gave him pause. "Listen, Miss Meadows. Lower the gun. I've never hit a woman before and I don't want to start now. So why don't you—"

"Stop doing that this instance!" Spoken like a true school teacher. Just one with a pistol now held straight at Zach's forehead. His upper torso froze in fear, but his feet seemed to take on independence and kept dancing.

"Zach, don't do anything stupid!"

"I'm warning you. Stand still!"

But Zach couldn't help it. Like a voice echoing at the end of a tunnel, the zone enveloped him. In for a dime…

Suddenly, Zora screamed, "Praise him!"

An involuntary reflex, Melora's gun hand shot up to Heaven. Zach grabbed her wrist and reached for the gun with his other hand. It came away easily. He danced back, forgetting about the pain in his throbbing foot. "Hah! Gotcha!" He hoisted the gun up and pointed it at Melora. "Now it's your turn to stand still!"

Melora kept her hands down. She sneered, wide and ugly and full of hatred. "If you think I'm going to jail, you're a bigger fool than I took you for."

"I'm nobody's fool, lady!" Not bad for a spur-of-the-moment catch phrase.

Zora said, "Give me the gun, Zach."

Zach looked her way. Just enough time for Melora to dart by him.

"Dammit!" Zach fumbled with the gun, got it up. But he couldn't shoot Melora, as much as she deserved it. Just couldn't do it. He aimed the gun up—Heavenward, just as Melora had done with her hand—and fired a warning shot. "Freeze!"

Blak!

"Not in the house, Zach!" he heard Zora scream.

Unlike in the TV shows, plaster dropped on his head from where he'd shot. He dropped like a sack of potatoes off the back end of a truck. He sat up, dizzy, then fell back again. White wisps of smoke curled around him, raising to Heaven. Maybe he shouldn't have shot the gun in that general direction. Revenge of the angels.

"She's getting away, Zach!"

From a distance, Zora's voice sounded warbly, one of his dad's hippy records played at a slowed-down speed. Outside a car beeped, a door clunked, an engine started.

"Dammit, Zach, give me your car keys!"

A hand was in his face now, the hand of God? No...Zora's hand. Something about car keys. He felt into his pocket, found them. Flung them up.

Then hit the floor.

Zora raced out of the house, keys jangling in her hand, cursing the stupidity of her brother. Of course he had managed to get the gun away from Melora. He'd just brought the house down doing so. Literally.

She jumped into the Trans Am, cursed Zach again. She kicked Styrofoam fast-food wrappers and sacks away from the gas and brake pedals. She couldn't believe he'd been driving that way, couldn't believe he'd put her at risk like that.

Down the street, Melora hightailed it at a risky speed. Her taillights glowed like demon eyes in the night. Zora backed down the driveway and slammed the gear into drive before the car stopped.

Grr-unk!

Car probably needed a new transmission anyway. She floored the pedal, swinging around the cars parked along the street. The speedometer hit 60 quicker than she expected, and Melora's taillights grew closer. She passed a school crossing sign with a 25 mph speed limit, grimaced, gave it a mental apology even though it was night.

Melora picked up her speed. A car came toward her, the headlights flashing from dim to bright as a warning. Recklessly, Melora aimed the car straight at the oncoming vehicle. For a second, Zora thought she intended to go out, suicide style. Except it'd probably be a no-no in her church's eyes. At the last moment, the other car swerved hard left, bumping over a curve and into a yard.

Zora knew she'd meant for the car to crash, to stop or kill Zora. Add it to Melora's list of crimes. She couldn't wait to make Melora pay for them. She smiled briefly at the thought and forced the power of that smile into her foot. 65 mph…

At the end of the block, Melora burst through a red light and turned. A car in the crossing lane screeched to a stop, horn blasting. Zora zipped around the corner, practically feeling the right tires lift. The she really let the gas fly. 70 mph, 75 mph…

She closed in on the tail end of Melora's car, a strong Caddy. Much more durable than Zach's tape and fast-food stitched-together vehicle. But she had to do it. Zach owed her money for damaging Phillip's car anyway. She took a chance, clipped the back end of the Caddy's bumper. The Caddy pulled right, whiplashed left. Zora slammed on her brake, digging down nearly to the floorboard before it took effect, let up. She flew out of her seat. Her head smacked into the windshield.

Thump!

The rebound tossed her back into her seat. Still going 65 mph. Then she looked up and saw a car bearing down on her. On instinct, she swung the wheel hard right. The back end skidded out, dropping her into a perpendicular to the road position. The approaching car braked. Tires screamed. Not enough. Like a rocket, she shot out of the car's path. The car clipped the back end of the Trans Am, righting it back into her own lane. And she hammered down on the gas.

Again, she narrowed the distance between them. This time, instead of bumping the car, she went over to the other lane, pushing it. The car shook, rattled as if coming apart at the seams. Zora's teeth chattered from the vibrations, her arms shaking wildly. She caught up, risked a wild glance over. Melora sat focused grimly behind her wheel, staring straight ahead and gripping the wheel like it was part of her skeletal system. Not exactly the satisfactory look of fear she'd desired. But Zora would make it come.

Now or never.

The ludicrous bird painted upon the Trans Am's hood cawed in her mind, mocking her.

Zora prayed; not a forced prayer, not a long drawn-out sermon from the mountain, just scared-to-death, desperate, hysterical gibberish.

Please don't let me die! I'll be nicer to people! I won't insult my brother! Sorry for some of the things I've said—I know God's "swear jar" is adding up—I can't die yet! I've got too much—

She cranked the wheel right.

Scrunchhhhhh!

Sparks flew up as she bounced off and ricocheted back into the tail end again.

Crunch!

Melora lost control, the Caddy serpentining back and forth across the road. Zora let up on the gas. The Trans Am grazed off the tail end with a horrible grinding sound, 10,000 dentist drills. The Caddy flew ahead, while Zora tore off into a tailspin. She spun around in a dizzying circle, hit the brakes again.

Screeeeee....

After a complete 180, the car stopped. Zora didn't, though. The car bounced, Zora wobbled. Her head spun, the nerve endings in her arms and foot tingling, racing like ants inside her bloodstream. Not far from her, the Caddy sat, stopped by a tree off the road. Smoke billowed out of the crunched-up hood. The car door opened. Melora's foot dropped out.

"Crap!" Zora tried starting the car, but it'd had enough. She snagged her gun from the purse, flung open the door and ran down the road. Like a drunk at a sobriety check point, Melora stepped out on unsteady feet. She staggered in a circle before spotting Zora. The image of Melora wavered in Zora's vision. But she saw her clearly enough to know she'd started running.

"Stop, Melora!" With her arms pumping, Zora managed to fire a shot into the sky. Melora halted, turned around. Then ran again.

Dammit! What's it take to stop this woman?

Zora dropped the gun into her purse and forced her legs to chop the pavement harder. Closer…closer… Exhausted, she jumped, hoping for a decent outcome. Otherwise she'd have to shoot the woman.

Too bad, so sad.

But luck finally dropped by. Zora fell short of her target, but reached out and snagged Melora's ankle. They both hit the grass. The gun bounced out of Zora's purse. The wind puffed out of her chest. Melora scraped fingernails into the ground trying to claw her way to freedom. Zora crawled up Melora's body, first the calves, the buttocks. Then she collapsed on top of her, wishing Melora'd give up already.

She didn't. She flung a fist back, nailing Zora in the jaw. Stunned, Zora fell back. With a hand on her jaw and blinking away lights, she said, "I can't believe you hit me, you bitch!"

Melora crawled to her feet, then crouched like a cornered wild animal. Pretty much hissed, too. "I'll do more than *that* to you."

Slowly, biding time, Zora got up. "Melora, do you really want to fight? The cops are gonna be here any second and it's kinda senseless at this point."

"You want some of *this*? I'll *never* give up!"

Of course she had to have a *you'll never take me alive, copper!* complex. Par for the course for Zora's day. The gun made more sense, an easier outcome than duking it out. But except for a sliver of moonlight, darkness had fallen. She'd be groping in the dark. Better than nothing. Zora turned, ran six feet. Her toe tapped into the purse. The gun had to be close by. She dropped in a squat, her hands searching the grass.

"What're you *doing*?" yelled Melora, uncertainty in her voice. Then, "Oh! You dropped your gun!"

Crunch, crnch, crinch…

Leaves snapped behind Zora. The footfalls grew louder, racing toward Zora. Zora flung an arm up in protective mode. Instead of flinging a fist to Zora's face, Melora dropped to her knees, crawling through the grass, searching.

"I'll find the gun first, you meddlesome feminist bitch! Then send you to Hell where you belong!"

"I may be a bitch, but I'm no feminist!" On second thought, Zora thought maybe she was. And proud of it. "So what if I am? Wanna test me?"

"God's on *my* side!"

"Thou shalt not murder!" Kinda felt good throwing scripture back at Melora, but the Charlton Heston movie was about as far as Zora's biblical education went.

Together, they performed a manic scavenger hunt in the dark. Leaves rustled beneath their groping fingers. A splinter from a fallen piece of bark bit deeply into Zora's fingertip. Her bones ached, her muscles needed rest. Far-off sirens cried out.

Zora nearly laughed at the ridiculousness of the situation. Working side by side, they could've been gardening instead of looking for a gun. Hysteria knocked at the back door of her brain. But she couldn't let it in, not yet.

Gotta keep searching…

Zora's fingers stumped into something cold, something unnatural in the grass. She didn't say a word, although she nearly let out a yip of victory. Time for that later. Quickly, she snatched it up, fumbled to get the handle in her grip. Cocked the trigger.

Click.

Zora stood, held the gun pointed toward Melora's dark figure. "*Now* will you give up?"

Melora said nothing. Then she stood. Dusted her hands. Her bony shoulders went up with a heavy sigh, then slumped down.

"Fine," said Melora, "but I could've whupped you in a fair fight."

"In your dreams, Melora." Childish, but the game had been won. Despite her full-length body ache, Zora smiled.

The cops had come and gone, no one more gleeful than Soundtrack Saul. "*Another case solvedddd, let's put it to restttt, look out bad guyssss, I'm nothin' but the besttttt! Ta-chaaaaa!*" Two murderers were now tucked away nicely in jail. Once again, Zora's brother had been cleared of any murder charges. To Zora's surprise, Zach's car actually fired up again.

"What's wrong, Sis?" They'd been quiet on the way to Zora's house, both clearly exhausted and loopier than a vaudeville comedian.

"Hm? Oh, nothing. No, that's not true. It's about Misty."

"Yeah, it sucks. She didn't deserve to die."

"No, she didn't. And while I don't agree with her experimenting in your beyond stupid Furries sex club, I—"

"Um, *not* my sex club."

"Whatever. I understand what drove her to it. What she'd told Melora. About not knowing who she is. And she never did. Nor will she ever. Because everyone tried to form her into their ideals, not taking into consideration what she wanted. In a way…I kinda understand."

"How's that, sis?"

"Well, don't get me wrong…I love Phillip and the kids…wouldn't take any of 'em back to the stork. But…growing up, I never really thought I'd end up as a baby-making machine."

"You're so much more than that, though. Really. You totes kick ass and—"

"Don't say 'totes.'"

"No, I'm serious, Sis. Earlier tonight, I was thinking how we pick at each other all the time, but that's 'cause we love each other. Kinda uncool to say it. But I'll say it anyway. I love you, Sis. And…I'm proud of you. Because you're Zora LeFevre, ace detective, super mother, awesome wife and kick-ass sister. And friend."

Zora looked at Zach, glad the dark night had fallen. Because like Zach, she didn't think it'd be cool to have him see her get all misty-eyed. He'd tease her mercilessly about it. She said nothing, just smiled.

"Gah! Listen to me, gettin' all sentimental and crap, Zor! Won't happen again. Hope you weren't recording this. Got a rep to maintain and all."

"You'll find out if I recorded your baby moment, Zach, when I get pissed off at you next. Now quit finding dead people. Please."

"Hey, they seem to find me. I know I'm attractive to living people...but dead people?"

She punched him in the shoulder. "Anyway...there really aren't too many who'll mourn poor Misty."

"That's not true. There's...our parents..." Zach taxed his brain, counting off his fingers again. Twice in one day. Maybe there was hope for him yet. "...Carlos and Della... Oh, crap! Carlos!"

Zora laughed. "Yeah, good luck when you release him. You might wanna step back."

"Wait...what? You don't think he'll go all psycho-pants on me, right?"

"Carlos? Probably not."

"Anyway...in his way, Martin Meadows would've mourned his wife. Um, if he was still alive."

"Yeah, there is that."

"Even Fireman Freddie." Zach's disdain showed with an upturned lip. "Creep that he is, he liked her. And then there's us. She was my friend. And you're mourning her."

Zach was right. Not that she'd ever say those ridiculous words. Zora'd never even met the girl, but felt she knew her. And she did mourn for her.

Zora pulled to the side of the road. Zach grabbed Zora's hand as they held a quiet, private memorial service for the late Misty Meadows. Whoever she may've eventually blossomed into.

Look for the next Zach and Zora Comic Mystery

NIGHTMARE OF NANNIES

About the Author

Stuart R. West is a lifelong resident of Kansas, which he considers both a curse and a blessing. It's a curse because...well, it's Kansas. But it's great because...well, it's Kansas. Lots of cool, strange and creepy things happen in the Midwest, and Stuart takes advantage of them in his work. Call it "Kansas Noir." Stuart writes thrillers, suspense and horror, both for adult and young adult audiences. Stuart spent twenty-five years in the corporate sector and now writes full time. He's married to a professor of pharmacy (who greatly appreciates the fact he cooks dinner for her every night) and has a twenty-six-year-old daughter who's still deciding what to do with her life. But that's okay. It took him twenty-five years to figure that out.

CROSSROAD
PRESS

www.ingramcontent.com/pod-product-compliance
Lightning Source LLC
LaVergne TN
LVHW091002080826
845145LV00003B/1098

* 9 7 8 1 6 3 7 8 9 6 1 7 4 *